BITSY'S
LABYRINTH

BITSY'S
LABYRINTH

MARY ANDONIAN

Kati:
Thanks for
supporting me!
Mary Andonian

Good Thief Press
Tualatin, Oregon

This book is a work of fiction. Any references to historical
events, real people or real locales are used fictitiously.
Other names, characters, places and incidents are
the product of the author's imagination, and any
resemblance to actual events or locales or persons,
living or dead, is entirely coincidental.

Library of Congress Control Number: 2010940670

Andonian, Mary.
Bitsy's Labrinyth/Mary Andonian.
Summary: Thirteen-year-old Bitsy Johnson describes the
summer her mom built a meditative walking labyrinth on
their lavender farm, and all the unexpected things that
happened to Bitsy because of it.

ISBN: 978-0-9831075-0-7 (paperback)

1. Teen—Fiction 2. Christian—Fiction
3. City and town life—Oregon—Fiction
4. Coming of Age 5. Inspirational

Cover design by Clark Kohanek
Interior design by Jennifer Omner

GOOD THIEF PRESS
Good Thief Press
PO Box 145
Tualatin, OR 97062-9210
Visit us at www.goodthiefpress.com

For my mom, Mary Lou Andonian
March 20, 1927 – August 9, 2006
"It's about baseball."

Contents

Contents

Contents

CHAPTER ONE

A Secret Visit

I HAMMER OUT my text with lightening speed: RU COMING OR WHAT?!

Maybe five seconds go by when my cell rings. It reads: IMPATIENT?

I look up and see Gina on the path in front of our house. She waves me down with her phone before tucking it in her pocket. Beside her, texting on her own phone, is Josie.

My cell rings again. This time it's from Josie. HURRY! It says.

I break into a jog to meet up with them. "Was this necessary?" I say, holding up my phone. "I'm looking right at you."

Josie smirks and puts away her phone.

We walk the path in the hot sun, past my neighbor's Christmas tree farm, toward town.

Gina says, "Have you told her yet?"

"My mom knows where I'm going," I reply.

"No, stupid," says Josie. "About your dad coming to Oregon."

"Not yet," I say.

"Why can't you ask Ellen to do it?" asks Gina.

"Are you kidding? My sister's words, and I quote: 'Not my plan, not my problem.'"

We trudge on. Josie's glasses slide down her nose. Gina tugs on her shirt to create a draft.

Josie asks, "When'd you see him last?"

"A year ago, when he married Coco."

"I thought you said her name was Charlene?" says Josie.

"Coco. As in coconuts?" I clarify, putting my hands to my chest to indicate Charlene is stacked. "They were practically spilling out of her slutty wedding dress. He's not even going to tell her. We're his," I air-quote for effect, "*customers* on a golf trip."

"That's brutal," Gina says.

I notice Gina's wearing a brand new outfit.

BLING is an understatement. I have to laugh. Like mother, like daughter.

"Gina," I say, "You could open in Vegas with that outfit."

"Gee, thanks. I'll take that as a compliment."

She smiles and moves ahead, and we all follow behind her for the next mile and a half. Gina's my best friend. And there's an unspoken understanding that she's the boss of our little posse.

I survived seventh grade and summer vacation is here at last. We're making our daily trek to the park. Last summer our town created a bike path that my friends and I call the Yellow Brick Road. Cheesy, I know. We each have direct access to this path from our driveways. Country living at its finest. Of course, my friends and I wouldn't be caught dead on a bike, but we like the path.

It's June, Summer Solstice to be exact, and Oregon's going through this sucky heat wave. It has to be the hottest day yet, and I feel like a sweat bucket by the time we make it to the park. Once there, I instantly recognize our other friends Dylan and Nick riding skateboards near the picnic tables.

Gina runs ahead when she sees Dylan. Josie makes a kissy face at me.

"There's your boyfriend, Nick."

"Shut up, Josie."

I grab my scrunchie from around my wrist and pull my hair into a ponytail. Only two more inches and I can cut it all off for *Locks of Love.* They make wigs for kids with cancer.

I hear Gina say to the guys, "We're going to the Zone! Want to come?"

The guys grab their skateboards to join us. I turn away to hide my smile.

CHAPTER TWO

The Zone

Nick and Dylan ride their boards in the parking lot next to the funeral home and cemetery—a place we've code named *The Zone*—while we walk through the gate.

In a grassy, shady spot, Gina sits on the ledge of an oversized fountain. Its water cascades from a tilted bucket held by a concrete angel. Gina flicks water on her legs. Without warning, she takes a scoop of water and flings it at Josie and me.

"Dude, stop!" yells Josie. "My glasses are getting wet!"

Josie thinks she's so cool in the latest frames. When she walks away to wring out her clothes, I say out of earshot, "Her freakin' glasses cost more than my computer."

"She acts like she'd be reading Braille without them," says Gina, "Why'd you say she could come?"

"I thought you invited her!"

We both sigh as Josie returns to the group, holding up a pack of cigarettes.

"You are so lucky they didn't get wet."

She pulls a cigarette from the pack and lights up. She grips it between hooked fingers and doesn't inhale. Why does she bother?

I pipe up, "Aren't those, like, ten bucks a pack?"

Josie laughs in a smug way, as if she's "All Knowing" on the price of smokes.

"Costs zippo. My mom stashes her cartons in the freezer." Josie eyes her lit cigarette, and adds, "I wish they were menthol."

Gina drags her hand along the top of the water again, but this time flicks the excess on her legs to cool herself. It's only eleven and already the sun is beating down on us. The heat wave is expected to last all week.

"I'm bored," says Gina.

"What else is there?" I ask.

"We could go for a walk on Bitsy's labyrinth,"

laughs Josie. She takes another clunky hit off her cigarette and looks at me expectantly. "Have you tried it yet?" she asks.

Here we go. I take a deep breath. "Um, that would be a no."

"When are you going to?" she presses.

"Let's see. I'm thirteen now, so that would be, like, *never.*"

Josie the Interrogator is relentless. "Why'd your mom get that thing anyway?"

"She likes the design."

Gina continues to drag her hand in the fountain water.

"What kind of design?"

Gina flicks some water at Josie, who looks irritated but doesn't do anything about it.

I break under the pressure. "It's a God thing, okay? What can I say. She likes props."

Josie bunches up her face like she just accidentally chugged sour milk.

Gina scoops a handful of water and throws it at her. "Hey, if it gets you a better hook up, why not? I suppose you're the self-reliant type."

Josie removes her glasses and wipes them with

the bottom of her tee-shirt. "Just because your mom's a Holy Roller, doesn't mean you can . . . "

I let out a loud shriek as cold water hits my legs. "Knock it off, Gina!"

I spin to give Gina the evil eye but instead see Nick and Dylan busting a gut next to the fountain.

Nick says, "Aw, c'mon, it's just water."

Josie flashes a smile at Nick. "Have you heard about Bitsy's labyrinth?"

"Latherinthe. Your mom a witch? Demon caller?" asks Dylan.

"That's *labyrinth*, you idiot," says Gina.

"I wish. She's not that cool," I say. Great. Now everyone's talking about me and my strange family. "It's sort of like a maze that you walk on. It helps clear your thoughts."

"What thoughts?" asks Dylan.

"Exactly," I say.

Nick stifles a laugh, and Dylan looks wounded when he finally figures out that I have just slammed him.

"Wow, harshed my mellow," says Dylan.

Josie says, "For real, does she channel spirits? Because I heard that girl . . . Megan? The one who died last year? She was into Ouija boards."

I'm beginning to lose it. "It's just a big hunk of cement. It does nothing, it *is* nothing. I can't believe she spent money on that when we could've had a swimming pool."

"We're getting a pool after Labor Day, when the prices drop," brags Josie.

Gina shoots Josie a dirty look. I glance over at Nick. He's watching me! I quickly look away.

This is going nowhere fast so I try a little diversion tactic. "Hey," I say, "did you guys check out Gina's new cell phone?"

Dylan takes the bait. He walks over to Gina who's proudly holding up a phone case with matching BLING, of course. Gina gives him the rundown on its many features while Josie crowds around them like a rock star groupie. Gina and Dylan are probably in the top five percent of the most popular kids at school. They're like a Sunshine Barbie set: Gina has long blonde hair and Dylan has short curly blonde hair, and they look like they belong in Southern California, and certainly not here in mainstream Oregon. Even though they're "just friends," everyone says that one day they'll probably get married.

Nick stays near me, however. "So the labyrinth," he says, "Is it like one of those mazes on the back of a cereal box?"

I'm about to answer when I spot a man, pushing sixty and wearing a cap and tweed jacket, walking among the rows of tombstones in the distance. The others follow my gaze and catch sight of him too.

"He's gotta be frying in those clothes," says Gina.

"It's the caretaker!" cries Josie.

The man stops in front of a headstone, looks down, removes his hat.

"Run!" I whisper.

Dylan and Gina are the first to bolt. Nick grabs his skateboard. Josie drops her cigarette in the fountain and sprints. Disgusted, I take it out and hold the soggy butt as if it's a slug as I run to keep up with the others.

CHAPTER THREE

Service Agent
for the Lord

I GO HOME and my mom's in the lavender field, pruning. We live on five acres of land in the Willamette Valley, two of which are my mom's lavender fields. That's how she makes a living: selling wholesale lavender to the surrounding nurseries and on-line to places all over the country. Everybody grows something around here. We also have an apiary—we call them bee boxes— on the back of our property that's managed by a local beekeeper, because it's a well known fact that where there's lavender, there are lots and lots of bees. He uses some of our land for the bee colonies, and in return the bees pollinate our lavender and we receive some yummy lavender honey. If you've ever tried lavender honey, you know it's a good deal. We've lucked out on the bees. They never disappeared from our farm like some of the other places.

I am grateful my mom grows something so beautiful and fragrant. It could be a lot worse. Josie's family has that alpacas farm and it stinks something awful. They're horrible creatures. One even tried to spit at me once when I got too close to it.

My mom sees me and waves me over. As I walk toward the lavender fields, I take a deep breath.

"It smells so good," I say as I reach her.

My mom laughs. "Four years later, and I feel the same way." She wipes her forehead with the back of her arm, and then points her pruning shears at the lavender. "Want to help cut back some of these? There's a ten in it for you."

"I'll take that bribe."

"Ellen would've held out for twenty."

"Where is she, anyway?" I ask.

"Inside. The heat's getting to her."

"That's lame."

She smiles. "Heads up. I'm meeting with Susan tonight so I won't be home for dinner."

I shrug, and look past the fields toward the labyrinth.

"We're going over a good story in the Big Book today. *Physician, Heal Thyself!* I knew the man who wrote it."

"Please don't start talking about all the important people you've met in AA. It gets kinda old."

My mom lifts her head and I can see her eyes beneath her U of O baseball hat. "Wow, that was unkind," she says.

"I'll go grab my gloves." I get up and walk away.

"Thanks for being of service!" she calls out.

"Whatever," I grumble and head toward the drying shed.

My mom LOVES God. Sure, she loves Ellen and me, but she REALLY loves God. Now that I'm thirteen, I have come to understand her special relationship with God for what it is. He did a good turn for her by helping her quit drinking in California, and she repays Him by doing things for Him every day. At least this is how I think it works. I know when she prays, she always says,

"Thank you, Lord, for keeping me sober today, and help me to do Your will always, Amen." They made a pact, an agreement. And this is why I'll never get hooked on alcohol or drugs or cigarettes. I don't want to have to become God's slave in order to have Him help me quit.

I walk to the drying shed. On the way I hear a faint buzzing sound from the apiary. The honeybees are fat and happy. During the Fourth of July weekend, we'll host our annual lavender festival, and this honey will be one of our biggest sellers.

Inside the shed are bundles of lavender hanging from the ceiling: some fresh, some dry. I spot my hat, gloves, and some Hefty bags near a bright red gas container; it smells nasty compared to the lavender. I move the container away from the lavender, grab my stuff, and head for the door. Instead of going back to my mom, I take a detour to the back of the shed. The buzzing gets louder as I make my way to the bee boxes. I stop and watch a few stragglers buzzing around the tops.

"Hey there," I say, holding out my hand to one of them. I watch it move around my outstretched fingers. "She used to read to me, you know," I whisper to the bee. It doesn't land.

I finally join my mom and her pruning. She takes great care to avoid the silver-gray flowers, instead focusing on the green brush beneath it. I follow closely behind, bagging the trimmings to make mulch out of it later.

"Do you know what today is?" I ask to make conversation.

"Wednesday?"

"Yeah, but something else."

"Oh, no. Have I forgotten something? I'm going out tonight. Please don't tell me . . . "

"Relax," I interrupt. "We don't have any plans. It's Summer Solstice."

"Summer Solstice! Of course," she sighs.

I brush a bee away from my leg. It moves in a jerky motion up, up, zigzagging in the air, and as it moves past my shoulders I can hear its faint brrrring sound, like a small windup toy that moves along some invisible surface.

"Are you going to be out late again?" I ask.

"I'm afraid so, but I'll make you some dinner before I leave." She gets a faraway look, then adds, "I'm so proud of her. She'll have sixty days on Friday. I remember sixty days as if it were yesterday."

I shake my head and chuckle.

"What's so funny?"

I stuff the trimmings in the bag. "Nothing."

"No, really. Tell me."

Another fat bumblebee does a drive-by near my ear; I fling my hand in the air, swing at it, and miss. I swing and miss one more time for good measure. Now if I just start muttering under my breath, I'll look like a *bona fide* crazy person.

I stand, brush dirt off my knees. "I said, nothing! Alright? Why don't you go adopt that stupid drunk if she means so much to you!"

My mom stabs her pruning shears into the dirt, and declares, "Elizabeth Ann Johnson, what has gotten into you?"

"I don't know. Never mind." I peel off my gloves. Ten bucks is *not* worth this.

"That woman needs a helping hand, the same way one was given to me when I was new."

I begin to recite the sentence along with her because I know it by heart and I wish to annoy her. She doesn't seem to notice. I look beyond her at the labyrinth. It adds a mystical elegance to the back of our property, I have to admit.

"We'll go out to dinner tomorrow night, how's that?" She asks.

"Great."

She shimmies off her gloves. "We'll stop and pick up a movie on the way home."

"Sounds good."

"Maybe even a little ice cream."

I smile. "You don't have to buy me off, Mom."

"Are you kidding? You're cheap. Ellen would've wanted a new wardrobe." She checks her watch. "Oh! I better get in the shower."

"I'll put this stuff away."

"You sure? I'd be very grateful," she says, and I know she means it. She breaks into a jog toward the house. "Love you, sweetheart!"

"Mom?" I call after her. "I need to tell you . . ."

She's already out of earshot. "Dad's coming to visit," I finish quietly. I see a bee pollinating a nearby lavender bush. I crouch down to eye level and say to the bee, "And he's leaving Coco and her Double Ds behind. What do you think of that?"

I pull out my cell, and text: CAN'T W8T 2 CU! XOXO

I look in the distance at the labyrinth on the other side of our property. I wonder if God knows how lucky He is to have my mom on His side. If

I told my mom this, she'd just say, "No, it's me who's lucky."

I don't believe it for a minute.

☙❧

I'M ALONE IN my bedroom, minding my own business and reading a magazine on my bed, when my obnoxious sister Ellen walks in.

"Don't you know how to knock?"

Ellen blows off my question. "Did you tell Mom yet?"

"You're the oldest. You should do it."

"I make it a point to never get involved. That way, it's never my problem."

Typical Ellen. "That is some great sisterly advice," I say.

"You better tell her soon, Bits. She's going to need the reaction time."

Ellen loves to eat, and it shows. She's two years older, and a good twenty pounds heavier. Who knows what will happen when she gets her driver's permit next month and Googles the nearest Krispy Kreme?

We're not quite total opposites: we both have my dad's dark hair and brown eyes, and that's pretty much where our similarities end. Ellen wears a size ten shoe; I'm a size seven. Need I say more?

She sits on the edge of my bed and begins sanding her nails with an emery board.

"You're doing it wrong," I say.

Ellen doesn't bother looking up, and continues to saw at her nails in a back and forth motion.

"I mean it, you're doing it wrong." I grab the emery board out of her hand. "See, you go in only one direction." I take the board and move it up the side of my nail, lift the board, and start at the bottom of my nail again. "Gina showed me."

Snatching the board back, she says, "I don't need beauty tips from children, thank you."

"Suit yourself. They're your nails." I go back to my magazine. It's no use arguing with Ellen. She always has to be right.

"Are you going to eat, or what?" she asks.

"I'm getting around to it."

"I'm going over to Michelle's after dinner so you're on your own tonight."

"And that's different from, say, every night this week?"

"Sarcasm doesn't suit you, Bits. Maybe you should take a twirl on Mom's labyrinth. Might make you feel better." She gets up to leave.

I won't even begin to talk about the labyrinth with Ellen. She knows how I feel about it. If it were up to me, I'd be doing cannonballs off our diving board in our brand new swimming pool.

"Are you staying over again?" I ask.

"Depends on how faded we get."

"Don't they notice the missing bottles?"

"Are you kidding?" Ellen laughs. "You should see their recycle bin."

"Sounds like Michelle's parents should hang out with mom."

She leaves. I put the book down and pull my knees to my chest. Ellen spends her nights drinking and staying away. Michelle's parents spend their nights drinking and staying away. At least on Wednesday nights. My mom spends her nights *not* drinking and staying away.

I spend my nights wondering why people don't stay.

CHAPTER FOUR

The Perfect Realtor

THE NEXT DAY Gina, Josie and I are walking down the Yellow Brick Road while Nick and Dylan skateboard beside us. We're all pretty sweaty. Josie takes a big hit off her cigarette and coughs. This makes me happy.

Josie says, "After swimming, we should all go try the labyrinth. Make a wish or something and see if it comes true."

"Um, sorry. It's under construction," I say, "My sister made a *huge* wish for what she wanted most in life, and it came true!" I pause for effect, and then say gravely, "It got crushed by a thousand donuts."

Josie scowls at me, which prompts me to add, "True story. Half chocolate, half glazed."

Gina laughs, "I can't wait to try it. Sounds like fun."

"It'll cost you," I say, "After we get it up and running again, I'm going to charge five bucks a spin. I'll let you know when it's open for business."

"Five bucks," says Dylan, "That's some serious bank."

Somehow Nick and I fall behind the group which causes another dirty look from Josie.

"You might as well show us," Nick says to me, "The lavender festival's next week. What are you going to do, put a sheet over it?"

I offer a stinging comeback. "You're so weird."

"It's good to try new things, Bits. Grows you as a person." He smiles at me.

My stomach flips and I look away. "Oh, and you're the grown person role model? Please."

I jog to catch up with the others, but not before I spot out of the corner of my eye that Nick's smile is growing wider.

When I catch up to Gina, I say, "It's times like now, when the humidity factor makes me want to throw up, that I am grateful to have friends with pools."

Gina shakes her head and laughs. Josie raises her head proudly, no doubt anticipating the day when she, too, will have her own pool and receive the gratitude.

Please.

We walk single file up to Gina's front door, passing her mom's SUV with the big ole Christian fish symbol slapped on its back. Once inside the house, we gather at the base of the stairs. I can hear Gina's mom, Mrs. Gallagher, upstairs talking to someone on the telephone.

"Mom, we're going swimming!" Gina shouts from the front of the line, and we all wait for confirmation that this is okay. I look around. On the living room wall is a jumbo crucifix and a velvet Jesus portrait, complete with encrusted jewels on the frame and dried palm reeds tucked behind one corner.

"Mom?" Gina calls again.

Just for sport I scan the walls for more crosses. There's one on the dining room wall, one in the hallway, one at the top of the stairs . . .

"Okay! Be careful! No rough-housing!" Mrs. Gallagher calls down to Gina.

We have confirmation.

After everyone has had a chance to change into their suits, we all hop into Gina's lukewarm pool, and I can't help but wish one more time that this is what my mom had spent Grandma's inheritance on instead of that stupid labyrinth.

Dylan does a handstand on the ledge, and slowly falls into the water. I notice Josie keeps a keen eye on Nick as he flips off the diving board.

As if on cue, Josie says, "Hey Bitsy, what's your mom going to build next, an altar?"

Without hesitation, I say, "Yeah, a Shamanic one. I'm going to drum my way to high school. I'll extract souls and sing Celtic songs. The super animals will guide me."

Gina smiles, clearly impressed by my quick wit and snappy reply. I wish it always came this easy for me.

Nick's got my back and adds, "I think the labyrinth sounds pretty cool."

Everyone looks at Nick as if he's grown a third arm in front of our very eyes. I can feel the heat rising to my cheeks so I take a quick dunk underwater, and pretend to be looking for something on the pool's floor.

When I finally come up for air, Nick is directly in front of me, smiling.

"When are you going to show it to me, Bits?" He says so only I can hear, and then he slips underwater and swims to the other side of the pool.

I look at the others. They silently stare at me. Finally, Dylan pipes up, "Bitsy's got a boyfriend."

"Shut up," I say.

"It's okay," says Josie, annoyed, "we won't tell anyone."

Gina quips, "You'd put it on the front page of *The Oregonian.*"

I climb out of the pool, wrap a towel around my waist, and make a beeline for the sliding glass door. "I have to go to the bathroom," I say.

Once safely inside the kitchen and away from the others, I towel dry my hair and body so I won't leave any tracks on the floor when I walk through the house. I hit the bathroom and on my way back I hear a muffled sound. I peek my head around the corner and spot Mrs. Gallagher at the kitchen table, wiping her eyes with a Kleenex.

"Oh! You startled me," she says. Her hand instinctively goes to the side of her head, as if primping her hair will make me forget that she was crying. Mrs. Gallagher is a Realtor, and if you ask me, Realtors always have perfectly sprayed hair with perfectly applied makeup, and they wear perfectly matched outfits. Mrs. Gallagher is the Perfect Realtor.

"Are you okay?" I ask, and I can't help but stare a bit. Mrs. Gallagher's face looks pale, despite the heavy makeup.

"I'm sorry, Bitsy, I didn't mean to scare you."

I follow her gaze to the cordless phone and the three wads of used Kleenex next to it. She continues, "I'm afraid I received some news today."

I hesitate. What do I say next? I finally stammer, "Uh, do you want me to get Gina for you?"

"No, that's okay." Her hand goes to the side of her hair again.

"Well, okay then . . ."

"So tell me about this labyrinth," she says, and now I'm really nervous, because it's a known fact that Mrs. Gallagher doesn't quite approve of my mom, but nobody talks about it and no one knows why. My guess is it's because my mom's a throwback from the sixties, and Mrs. Gallagher is not only a Perfect Realtor, but she's also CONSERVATIVE.

"That's what it is, alright."

"Yes, I know. I asked you to tell me about it."

I shrug and smile. Whenever a kid is in a bind, it's always best to shrug and smile. She smiles back and I know it's a fake. I take it as my cue to leave.

"Wait," she says.

I turn, I shrug, and I smile again. What else is there to do?

"Is your mother part of any, you know, associations?"

"I'm not sure I understand."

"It's common knowledge she attends a twelve step program."

"So much for anonymity, huh."

"I do know all about them, you know," she sniffs. "Our church sponsors one of the meetings on Thursday nights. That's tonight."

"I guess."

"Does your mother attend church?"

"We don't . . . she doesn't."

"Does she consider herself a Christian? Because

I thought she was, but then I heard about this labyrinth . . . "

"Maybe you should ask my mom."

I feel like I've stepped into a camouflaged trap and at any moment the hidden rope will wrap around my foot and I'll instantly go upside down in the air.

"I didn't think so." She pats the side of her head again.

"She, uh, does other things."

Mrs. Gallagher purses her lips. I give a thumbs up to the sliding glass door. "I think I'll go hit the ole diving board again."

"Certainly, dear."

I have just participated in the Catch and Release program.

I turn to leave, but Mrs. Gallagher stands.

"Bitsy."

Our eyes meet, and she continues, "Please don't say anything about this to Gina. She'll just worry."

I'm a bit clueless as to what she means, so I just shrug and smile. "Sure. No problem."

I quickly head outside before she can stop me again. And I thought I had a kooky mom. Sheesh!

CHAPTER FIVE

It's a Labyrinth

I GRAB MY clothes off the lawn chair and wiggle them on over my bathing suit. Everyone's watching me from the pool.

Gina asks, "Where you going?"

"I forgot about something."

"Dude, take a joke," says Josie. "I'll stop messing with you, alright?"

I wave them off and head home.

I'm a good block away from Gina's house on the bike path when I hear something behind me. It's Nick, carrying his clothes and riding his board.

"Slow down, will you?" he calls.

I slow my walk to a straggle and try to hide my nervous smile. Nick stumbles as he pulls his clothes on over his swim trunks. He skates up to my side.

"What happened back there?" he asks.

"Nothing. I forgot I had to help my mom with the festival."

"I'm coming with you."

This is *definitely* unexpected.

He bolts ahead of me on his skateboard and I can't help but notice how he flexes his leg each time he pushes against the Yellow Brick Road to increase his speed. Soon he's way ahead of me and I take a deep breath to calm myself.

We get to my house and my mom's goofy bike with the metal basket is propped up against the garage. This is her contribution to the "green" movement. I open the side gate and we sneak along the side of the house toward the backyard. When we get there, I raise my fingers to my lips, motioning Nick to be quiet.

My mom is walking the labyrinth.

"Why's she moving so slow?" Nick whispers.

"That's how you do it," I take a deep breath, and then add, "She talks to God while she walks." I cannot believe I just said that out loud.

From the way Nick looks at me, I feel like he

somehow understands, because he doesn't crack a joke or run away.

We watch as my mom quietly walks along the curved path, its paver stones a lighter gray than the border. The entire labyrinth is a circle the size of a full-sized swimming pool. My mom is looking down with her hands behind her back.

Nick says, "Looks like she's enjoying the conversation."

"Yep, she loves that God alright."

"Jealous?" asks Nick.

I don't show it but, truth be known, I guess I *am* jealous.

And then I fall. My foot catches on Nick's sneaker and I take a nose dive into the gravel next to the barbecue grill.

I hear my mom calling in the distance. "Bitsy?"

Before I can recover, Nick pulls me back up by my shoulders and I feel myself flush. Next thing I know, my mom's brushing dirt off my knees.

"Are you okay?" she asks.

I nod. Nick clears his throat. "Hey, Mrs. J."

I like that Nick calls her "Mrs." and not Amy-Beth, like all of my other friends.

"Hello, Nick," she nods to him. She sizes me

up. "You look guilty of something. What's going on?"

"Nick was going to help me back here but then we saw you."

"You looked busy, Mrs. J."

My mom smiles at Nick. I think she likes Nick because of our California Connection: His family moved here from California the same year we did when my parents got divorced. Nick and I were the new kids in the fourth grade, and have been friends ever since.

My mom motions for us to follow her back to the labyrinth. I am mortified, to say the least. When we arrive at the foot of the opening, she says, "Do you know how old labyrinths are, Nick?"

"I know you got yours a couple a days ago."

My mom's blue eyes sparkle. "They've been around a long time, some dating back to over forty-five hundred years. In our culture, the Hopi Indians had a symbol for Mother Earth known today as the 'Classical Seven-Path Labyrinth'."

"That's what we have," I sigh.

Nick studies the swirling path in front of him. I knew it would go like this. My mom will talk him to death and then we'll have to bury him in the lavender field. I can only imagine Nick's body would make great mulch.

My mom continues, "Labyrinths were made near sacred places to remind us that we are connected to nature and to God. When you walk a labyrinth, you are really taking time to say, 'Thank you' to your Creator and to consider the divinity in all things."

"Divinity?" repeats Nick, like he's never heard the word before.

My mind reels. C'mon, mom! Why can't you just be a normal mom in a normal town, talking about normal things? How about: How's your horseback riding going, Nick? Or let's try: How're your parents, Nick? But no, it has to be . . .

"Yes, the divine, the Godliness in our world." My mom smiles knowingly at Nick, who now stares at the labyrinth as if it's about to glow.

"I want to try it," I say, pointing to the center of the labyrinth. "That's where you're supposed to dump your problems, but how can I get Josie to stay there?"

Nick grins and shakes his head. My mom reaches over and gives me a squeeze. I go rigid at her touch.

"What I like to do is spend the time walking toward the center thinking about the problem, and then when I get to the center, I say, 'God, I am giving this to You, okay?' And then when I walk away, I leave that problem in the center, behind me."

Nick blinks a few times. I can tell that the engine called Nick's Brain is beginning to sputter and steam. I slink out of my mom's grip.

"I, uh, gotta go," Nick says.

"Would you like to try it sometime?" My mom asks Nick.

My eyes grow wide and I mouth the words "shut up!" to my mom.

"Yeah, sure," says Nick.

Nick and I say our good-byes and leave the same way we came. Just before closing the gate, I turn one last time to see my mom waving at us.

"Bye! Come back soon!" she calls.

When we get to the front of the house, Nick pushes his skateboard off to a start, and says, "Whoa, your mom's pretty out there."

"I know," I call out to Nick, who is already on the bike path. When he's out of sight, I turn an angry eye toward the house. Boy do I ever.

ℭℛ

I'VE GOT MY arms firmly crossed in front of me, waiting for my mom to finish her walk on the labyrinth. She's completely self-absorbed and only notices me as she reaches the end.

"Thanks a lot! Now he thinks I'm a mutant because of this stupid thing."

"Aren't you being a bit dramatic? He looks like he was very interested."

"Yeah, that glazed look in his eyes just screamed excitement."

My mom gives me a sympathetic look, which makes me even angrier.

"I wasn't going to say this in front of Nick," she begins, "but I'm afraid I've got some bad news. I can't do dinner tonight."

Unbelievable.

"I am so sorry. I had my dates wrong. Susan has sixty days *today*, not tomorrow. I have to go to the meeting. I'm her sponsor. I can't miss it."

I cross my arms even tighter, to the point of hugging myself.

"But we'll do it tomorrow night, okay? It's just a matter of switching days."

I stare at the labyrinth, listening.

"Bitsy?"

I look at my mom and nod. "Fine," I say, "I don't really care."

My mom smiles and puts a hand on my shoulder.

"Tomorrow will be a lot of fun. I'm really looking forward to it."

I pull away and walk toward the patio. "Whatever," I say under my breath.

CHAPTER SIX

Dylan and the Ninja

IT'S FRIDAY MORNING. I pull out my cell phone as I wait in the driveway for my friends. I text: DAD, U THERE? XO B.

I wait, staring at my phone, hoping to get a response. Nothing. Next, I text Gina: HURRY!

I look up and sure enough, Gina is walking past the bottom of my driveway, looking down at her phone. She looks up at me, and shakes her head.

Gina's in another loud outfit and, as usual, it looks perfect on her. Like Realtor, like Realtor's daughter. I run down my driveway and slide into a walking stride next to her.

"Did you tell her yet?" asks Gina.

"No, and stop asking!"

We spend the next ten minutes walking and texting everyone we can think of. When we walk past the park without stopping, I ask, "Where're we going?"

"Dylan's," Gina replies and giggles like she's still in the 7th grade. It's *so* last year.

"Why are we going over there?"

"He wants us to see a new video game he got this week. Nick will be there," she adds, giggling again.

I look up at the sky to see how I should feel about staying indoors today to watch video games. It's something I've done ever since moving here from California. If the sky is gray, and it usually is, then I don't have to feel guilty about staying inside. But if it's a nice day, sunny or partly cloudy, then I am wasting a perfectly good day if I stay indoors.

Thank goodness the sky is gray. Bonus: It's hot and muggy, too.

Gina knows my logic, so she says, "It's going to rain any minute . . . what else is there?"

I consider this. Not a whole heck of a lot. "Okay, but let's not stay too long."

"Why, what's on your busy agenda?" Gina asks.

"Nothing, really."

"What's 'nothing, really'?"

"My mom's taking us out to dinner tonight."

"That's great," she says dubiously.

We stop in front of Dylan's house. Before knocking on the door, we each pull out a lip gloss and use it.

Gina knocks three times before we decide to let ourselves in. We find Dylan and Nick in the family room, frantically pressing buttons on a video game controller, one in each hand, and shouting at Dylan's big screen TV to GET OUT OF THE WAY!

Gina sits on the couch next to the guys and I instantly feel out of place. Nick takes his eyes off the screen and says "hi" to me. He must pick up on my vibes because he quickly hands the controller over to Gina so she can take his place. She's psyched, but Dylan says, "Great, now we're going to get mutilated beyond recognition."

"What kind of a game is this?" asks Gina.

I reply, "If it's something Dylan likes, then it has to be disgusting."

"You know it," Dylan grunts proudly before continuing his game. On the TV screen, a Ninja draws a sword. Dylan barks at Gina, "Don't touch anything!"

Gina throws down the remote and sinks into the couch to watch Dylan on his game.

Nick gets up and moves toward me. "Want something to drink?"

Before I can say anything, Dylan and Gina shout, "Sure!" I laugh and stare at my shoes.

Dylan ducks as if he's in the game, and then hits the remote's pause button. The image on the TV is frozen as Dylan frantically thumbs through a Ninja Guide Book for direction. "Red Bull!" he calls, without looking up from his book.

"I can help," I say.

As Nick and I go to the garage, I glance back to see Gina winking at me, and mouthing the words, "Go for it!" I turn to Nick and realize he caught the whole thing. I feel my eyes grow to epic proportions.

"That's all we need," says Nick as we walk through the house toward the garage.

"What's that?"

"Dylan all pumped up on Red Bull playing that Ninja game."

"Oh," I say, relieved.

"That, and everyone thinking something's going on with us."

I giggle and it comes out a snort. How feminine of me. "It looks like you were into it." When he grins, I quickly add, "The game! You were into the game."

"The game's just okay."

I smile, shyly. Since when do I feel shy around Nick? Nickeroo? The Nickster? "So what games do you like?" I ask.

"I like the wii, and all that. But I like there to be more to it than maiming people. I like mystery games."

"Tell me more. It sounds so mysterious." I crack myself up.

Nick smiles at me like I'm the dork that I am. "They're the kind of games where you have to make choices and solve puzzles before you can get ahead. You have special powers and there's usually a dark force that tries to stop you. You know, fantasy."

I exaggerate my nod to show how much I get his description. Then I say, rather proudly, "I'm a Boggle girl myself."

Again, the dork kindness smile. "That doesn't surprise me."

"Why do you say that?"

"You're very traditional."

"And what would that mean?"

"It's a good thing."

Nick opens the fridge and pulls out four Red Bulls.

"Water for me, please."

He puts back two cans and pulls out two water bottles. With a smile, I take the two waters from him. At the garage door, we both linger for a second before Nicks opens the door for me. Bowing, he says, "After you."

Chivalry is *so* not dead.

CHAPTER SEVEN

Boggle Girl

ONCE BACK IN the family room, I spot Gina nudging Dylan as if we're the new entertainment.

"What?" says Dylan, completely engrossed in the video game.

Gina gives him a look like "Are you clueless?" She smiles at us as we hand off the drinks.

Nick says, "Dude, do you have any board games?"

"Bonus Room," says Dylan, barely looking up.

Nick smiles at me and my heart falls into my shoe.

We go upstairs to find the games and, sure enough, there's Boggle. He plucks it off the shelf.

"We should bet something," I say.

"Winner chooses," he says flirtatiously.

OMG.

We play, and I'm happy to report that Nick's a worthy opponent. I hold a pad of paper while Nick ticks off the last of his words.

"Pie?" he reads.

"I can't believe I missed that one. It was such a lame word, too."

"I have five unique words, my friend."

"Oh? I have pier, press, lip, ate, piers and pierce." I straighten a bit. "That would make me the winner."

Nick throws his paper and pencil up in the air in mock frustration. "Oh, no."

"Hmmm. I'm kind of low on cash," I say, scratching my head.

"At least I was close. Didn't think I was that smart, did you?" he asks.

"I think of you as—how can I put this—quasi-smart."

"You think I'm brilliant."

"Quasi! Semi. Partial. Not quite."

"So you're saying I'm a genius."

I laugh. "Yes, yes, okay? In an Einstein-looking way, sure."

"Are you referring to my hair?" Nick runs his fingers through his messy black hair.

"More like your guppy eyebrows."

"My what?"

"I don't know how my family started it, but we call hairy Einstein eyebrows 'guppy eyebrows.'"

"I didn't know guppies had eyebrows," he says, moving his eyebrows up and down. It's hilarious, and I can't help but laugh.

"You think that's funny, do you?" He grabs my hands and holds them behind my back and starts tickling me while he bunches up his eyebrows some more. I am laughing so hard now that I can't breathe, and I am also excited because Nick is so close to me and his hand feels strong against my hands. The grip is tight, but not so much that it hurts.

And then he stops tickling me, but he still has his arm around me and his hand is still grasping mine, and he just looks at me. I hold my breath. Is this it? Is this the moment I will always remember as My First Kiss?

"What's going on here?" Mrs. Gallagher declares from the doorway.

Nick drops his hands.

Dylan and Gina crowd behind Mrs. Gallagher. Dylan mouths the word, "SWEET!" behind Mrs. Gallagher's back.

Only Dylan would find this moment amusing.

"I . . . he . . . what do you mean?" I say, flustered beyond belief. Nick makes a bee-line toward the crowd at the doorway.

"I don't think it was a trick question." She smiles at Nick. "Perhaps you can enlighten me?"

"We were playing Boggle! And there were guppies . . . and that was it!" he says.

"It's true," I say. "I have to go now." I run past the others and take the stairs two at a time.

Mrs. Gallagher and Gina are right behind me. Gina silently waves goodbye to Dylan. As they pass by me, Mrs. Gallagher and I briefly make eye contact. She looks disappointed, and it makes me feel terrible.

We all watch through the picture window as Mrs. Gallagher and Gina get into their black SUV and take off without looking back.

"What was that?" asks Nick.

Dylan slouches back into the couch and picks up the game controller. "They needed to get back cuz her dad was on some early flight."

"I wonder if he's okay," I say.

"My guess? They're breaking up," says Dylan, already picking up where he left off in the game. "You think they're the perfect family on the outside, but those are the ones who wind up going locomotion in the cabaña."

I try to shake off Dylan's stupidity. "Is English your second language or something?"

Dylan makes his Ninja warrior do a virtual back kick. "You know, crazy stuff . . . divorce, murder, things like that."

Nick pipes up, "Dude, you are such a tool. Bitsy's parents are divorced."

Dylan is completely unaffected. Instead, he dodges arrows by moving the controller in the air. "Damn! Almost got nailed there." He makes a mock-leveling of the controller, before saying, "Sorry, Bits. No harm intended."

"No harm taken, Dylan. After all, I have to consider the source."

CHAPTER EIGHT

Bad News

THE DARK CLOUDS move fast in front of the gray sky. The rain comes as a light drizzle.

I practically jog The Yellow Brick Road all the way home, ignoring the park completely, even though we said we'd stop there on the way back. What fun is it now when you're a singular sensation?

As I reach my house, Ellen's coming out the front door with her friend, Michelle. Michelle is overweight like Ellen, only she tries to compensate by wearing a hideous nose ring. They hop into Michelle's car, a Volvo that's nicer than my mom's, and back out of the driveway.

"Wait! Where's Mom?" I say, running to catch up with them. Michelle brakes.

"How should I know? She went to meet someone for lunch about a half hour ago."

"What about you?"

"Michelle and I are going to hang out at her house for awhile."

As the car moves down in the street, I yell, "Don't forget about tonight!"

"Ha! I won't forget, but I bet Mom will," Ellen says, and then shouts out the window, "Get ready for leftovers!"

It stopped raining, so I walk around the garage to get in through the back door. Before I go inside, though, I make a stop at the opening of the labyrinth. It really is pretty cool. It looks so ancient, and yet so new at the same time. I can see why my mom placed it here. As you walk, you can see the potted flowers all around the path, but if you look ahead in the distance, you can see the lavender farm. If you come outside at just the right time, you'll see the sun set behind the lavender. I have to admit, if there is a God, He shows up every single night in the sunset over our lavender farm.

I step onto the labyrinth. A bee hangs in the air nearby. "I can't pray to save my life," I say to the bee.

Are you there, God? It's me, Margaret. Just kidding. It's one of my favorite Judy Blume books. Uh, you know that.

I look up at the sky. Rain clouds move over my head. Man, this praying business is the worst. I really have a hard time concentrating.

Um, okay, God. I've got real problems. Could you please help me solve "the dad" issue? I'm on a tight deadline. Like, tomorrow. So if I could get just ten minutes of uninterrupted time with my mom, I'm sure I can explain everything. So just give me some time, okay? And while we're at it, I don't get why she has to be gone all the time to help people. What about me? I'm a people. Uh, you know what I mean. I may not look like I need helping, but what about my sister? Look at her. She's always mean to me and is very sarcastic to Mom, and I just wish she would be nicer to me.

I debate whether or not to mention that Ellen drinks with Michelle but then realize if God was capable of making the universe, chances are He knows about Ellen. *What a know-it-all*, I think, and then chuckle at my witty one-liner.

I continue walking in silence. The rain is still drizzling like one of those theme park water misters, and it feels good on my arms and legs. This heat wave is getting old, and it's supposed to stay this hot and muggy for another week. I wish I was swimming in a nice, big swimming pool, instead of walking on this stupid thing.

I continue to pray: *And, God? What about Nick? He's been my friend since forever and now all of a sudden he acts all googly toward me. It really freaks me out. I like him as a friend, but* . . .

Immediately I feel a big pang of guilt, because the truth of it is that I do like Nick, and I wanted him to kiss me today, and here I am complaining to God about Nick. As if He didn't see exactly what happened today. *The know-it-all.* Suddenly this concept doesn't seem so funny anymore.

I stop at the middle and look at the back of our house. Everything is still and quiet, except now the mist has turned into a soft rain and I can hear it drain down the gutter spouts and drip onto the back patio.

I begin the walk back through the maze, speeding up as I do so. Am I supposed to be contemplating God's answer to my prayers? Probably. But am I? Not a chance. I'm thinking about my dad and Coco the Wonder Whore, Nick and his guppy eyebrows, my big, fat drunk sister, Ellen, and how my mom's never home. And even though I'm thirteen, I still don't like to walk into the house alone, and I wish God would just be done with my mom already.

"Hey, God," I say out loud. "Hasn't she done enough for You, yet? How many people does she have to help stop drinking before You'll leave her be!"

"Bee! OW!" I manage to step on a huge bumble bee and it stings me squarely in the arch of my foot. I shake my foot violently and there's no need to mutter under my breath, because now I really do look like a *bona fide* crazy person. I've had my share of bee stings, but this is the first time I've actually *stepped* on a bee.

"Great! Is this my answer to prayer? You sting me? Well, who needs you, anyway!"

I limp off the labyrinth, doing a fancy little peg-leg walk by walking on the heel of my throbbing foot. I hop inside the house, grab a seat at the kitchen table, and take a look at the bee sting. The stinger fell off, thankfully. In its place is a nice swollen ring the size of a dime, thick around the dot where I got stung. My mom showed me how to make a baking soda paste for bee stings, but now with our lavender taking off, I've been stung so many times I don't even bother putting anything on it. I know the drill. Everything returns to normal after an hour or two.

After the bee sting episode, I spend the afternoon treating myself to some downtime. I read books, listen to music, and eat. Well, graze, actually. I never manage to eat an entire lunch in one sitting, but instead have something every fifteen minutes: two slices of cheese, a bagel, a glass of strawberry milk, a handful of cashews, and some potato chips. I'm getting ready to break out the gummy worms when my phone vibrates.

Excited, I reach for the phone. I'm disappointed to see the text is from Gina and not my dad.

"I need 2CU."

"Come on over."

"Thx SYL."

Ten minutes later, Gina's at my front door. Her eyes are swollen and red.

"Let's go to my room."

Gina zips past me upstairs. Already my bee sting is just a mild irritation. I barely feel it as I take the stairs behind her.

In my bedroom, Gina is on my bed with her arms crossed behind her head. I follow her eyes to the underside of my canopy where I have a school photo of Nick tucked underneath the frame. I snatch it down and throw it behind the bed.

"I don't know how *that* got there," I say.

Gina simply smiles at me in understanding.

I plunk down on the bed next to her. "I thought you had to go pick up your dad."

"We did."

"What's going on?"

"I am seriously freaking out."

"Did you and Dylan break up?"

"No, I almost wish."

"Then what is it?"

Gina's eyes well up. "My mom has cancer. The weird kind of blood cancer that old people get."

"But your mom's not old."

"I said the exact same thing! It's crazy. And my dad? He came home early from his business trip, and he *never* skips work."

Gina breaks down then, rolling over and turning into a ball. I have no idea what to do so I do the clunky "pat on the shoulder" thing. She startles me when she grabs my hand and clutches it for dear life.

She rolls over to face me. "I was thinking . . . maybe if I walked your labyrinth."

I pull my hand away and consider her request. Finally, I say, "About Ellen's wish . . . I was just kidding about those donuts."

Gina's expression has "DUH" written all over it.

So I shrug, and say "Sure, what do you got to lose?"

CHAPTER NINE

Friday Night Slight

I OPEN THE back door and the summer heat instantly closes in on us and I am surprised for a moment by its intensity. It's easy to forget that Oregon's having a big ole heat wave when you're downloading songs off iTunes in your air-conditioned bedroom.

I walk Gina to the base of our labyrinth. She just stands there looking confused.

"Okay, then," she says.

"You need to walk it."

"I know THAT part. Then what?"

I say in my best munchkin voice, "Follow the yellow brick road."

"I'm waiting for the lightning bolt, Bits," says Gina, looking up at the sky.

"No, seriously, see the center there? That's where you're going to put your mom's cancer."

"How do I do that?"

"You make it up as you go. You can stomp on it, throw it, heck, you can drop kick it if you want. The point is when you put her cancer in the middle, God will take it from there. At least according to my mom."

"This was a bad idea. I don't know what I was thinking."

Gina turns to leave, but I feel committed so I stop her. "What else do you got?"

"I'm going to look stupid," she says, wiping sweat from her forehead.

I take a deep breath. "I have a confession to make." I look over my shoulders to make sure no one's listening. Gina stares at me intently.

"Maybe God *is* like Santa Claus," I say. "My mom's living proof that you can bargain with Him on stuff. She asked Him to help her stop drinking and He did. So she pays Him back by helping others. It's pretty simple."

Gina shakes her head. "That's the problem. I do think God is like Santa Claus, as in . . . "

"But your mom's a bible thumper!"

"Just cuz my family goes to church doesn't mean I believe that stuff. What if it doesn't work?"

"Guess you'll never know unless you try."

She lets out a yelp as I push her to start. She looks back at me, irritated.

Gina walks as if on a tightrope, foot over foot, sometimes teetering a bit. She even holds her arms out straight to balance herself. I stand on the side of the labyrinth and watch. No way am I getting back on that thing.

Gina hops over the bee that stung me. I give it the look of death.

At first, I'm skeptical. Gina looks resigned to just go through the motions. I continue to focus on Gina's walk: one step in front of the other, wobble-wobble. I find myself leaning when Gina leans as if I am on the tightrope with her.

Eventually her face becomes more solemn, intense. Suddenly she stops.

"What's the matter?" I ask.

"I feel something," she says.

"What is it?"

"I think I feel God."

"What does He feel like?"

"He feels calm."

"Are you sure it's not just you who feels calm?"

Gina considers this, and shakes her head. "Never mind."

And then, just like that, she starts walking again. So Gina gets to feel God and I get to feel guilty for not talking to God in just-the-right-way, and I wonder what it's going to take to really get to know this God, anyway.

☙❧

LATER, AT THE base of my driveway, Gina says, "Thanks, Bitsy."

"No charge."

Gina laughs, "That is so spiritual of you."

I wave until I can no longer see her on the Yellow Brick Road, and then go inside and slouch on the couch for my daily exercise of channel surfing.

I am FAMISHED. I can't wait for my mom and Ellen to come home so we can go to dinner.

It's already a few minutes past five, and if we leave quickly we can avoid the Friday night crowds. I think about the movie I want to rent: Something light and fun that doesn't have to do with God or cancer or guys or anything remotely resembling real life. This is really going to limit my options.

The garage door opens so I run to the back door.

"Relax, it's just me," Ellen says.

"What took you so long?"

As I try to move toward Ellen, she backs away and I instantly know why. She smells like cigarettes. "Did you smoke?" I ask. Ignoring me, Ellen quickly walks through my mom's bedroom and into her bathroom. I follow behind.

I ask again, "Were you smoking?"

She snatches the toothpaste off the counter and spins toward me. "Michelle smokes, not me." She squeezes a dab of toothpaste on her finger and smears it on her teeth. She swishes it in her mouth, spits it in the sink, and says, "Mom's not here yet, is she?"

"What if she was? We'd be waiting on your stupid face!"

I storm off but not before I catch the slightest hint of sadness on Ellen's face. Maybe she does care, after all.

I go back to the couch and listen to Ellen's side of a phone conversation in the kitchen.

"Hi, is my mom there? Thanks." Ellen pauses, and then, "When are you coming home? Dinner? Ring any bells? With your kids?"

Another long pause.

"Sure, Mom. I get it, I get it. Got it covered."

The phone slams in its cradle. Ellen pokes her head around the corner.

"What did I tell you," she says.

I wait for an explanation.

With a theatrical back-of-the-hand to her forehead, she says, "The drunk lady really needs me tonight! She's alone with her kids and wants to get loaded!" Ellen winks at me and saunters off.

"So who cares?" I shout. "Let her!"

Ellen calls from the kitchen, "Hail, Bitsy, full of grace."

I follow her to the kitchen where Ellen's rummaging through the fridge.

"Don't you remember our little adventures to the liquor store?" she says without looking up.

"Oh, so now you're going to defend mom? She hasn't been home one night this week!"

"And you ain't grateful? Man, Bits, you are one needy little kid."

If I had a cat, I would've thrown it across the room. Not really, but still. I can't talk to this sorry excuse for a sister. I consider various ways of killing her. No use. I would never get away with it.

"What's it going to be, creep? Pizza or Lean Cuisine?"

Let's rethink this. How can I get away with it? There's poison. There's death by blunt object. Or sharp blade. IT WAS BITSY IN THE KITCHEN WITH THE WEED WACKER.

No, that won't do. I squeeze my eyes shut: *Okay, Lord. Help me out here. I'm ready to take out one of Your own.*

"Bitsy!"

I open an eye to see Ellen glaring at me. In her left hand is a thick, triangular piece of foil; in her right, a box of Lean Cuisine.

"Pizza," I say.

"Good." She slaps the triangle-shaped foil on the counter. "Dinner's served."

I nuke the pizza too long, and as I eat the

chewiest Take-n-Bake ever, I find myself wondering how Gina managed to use the path and make it work for her, when she didn't believe in it any more than I did. Does God reveal Himself on a "need to know" basis? Who's to know?

CHAPTER TEN

The Situation

TWENTY MINUTES LATER, Ellen is watching *Wheel of Fortune* and I'm practically licking my container of Ben & Jerry's Cherry Garcia, when the phone rings. I check out the number and don't recognize the area code so I almost don't pick it up, but then it occurs to me it's a Seattle exchange. I quickly lift the receiver on the third ring.

"Hello?"

"Is that you, Ellen?"

"Dad! It's me, Bitsy," I say joyfully.

"Bitsy! How's my itsy spider doing?"

He laughs a little too long. I instantly go on guard.

"Fine, dad. How are you? How's Seattle?"

"Seattle's perfect. Perfect weather, perfect week. Perfect. Oh, and I got the deal at Boeing, so that's perfect too."

In the background, I hear people talking loudly and when he mentions Boeing, they get louder. It sounds like he's in a crowded room and judging by his voice, I'd say that crowd was in a bar. "Wow, that's great," I offer. "Congratulations."

He laughs again and has a side conversation with someone in the background. I wait a reasonable amount of time before saying, "Dad?"

He calls out to someone that he'll take another, and then returns to the phone by saying, "Bitsy, is that you?"

"Still here, dad."

"Listen, I have bad news."

I close my eyes and try to squeeze out the memory that wants to surface to the top of my thoughts. With all my might, I push it down. Way down. I don't want to remember that. Please.

"What's that," I finally say.

"I need to get back to California. Char's mom decided to fly in from Texas and she really wants me to be there. I can't tell her a golf trip is more important than her mother, can I?"

The memory is persistent. It wants to be played. I won't let it.

"Maybe if you told her the truth."

He breathes a heavy sigh. "Sweetheart, you don't understand the situation. I can't cause any waves right now. It's tough enough as it is."

I remain silent.

"I'll reschedule the golf trip for next weekend, alright? We'll just back it up a week."

"But next week's the festival."

The bar noise swells.

"What? I can't hear you."

I'm about to repeat myself when I reconsider. Why not next weekend? It's not like I have to work the festival the entire weekend. And maybe this way my mom will be too preoccupied to even know he's in town. I say loudly, so he can hear me over the bar noise, "Never mind. Next weekend sounds great!"

"Terrific."

"So what else is . . . "

"Gotta run, Honey," he interrupts, oblivious. "I'll catch up later."

"I love you, Dad," I say, but he doesn't hear me. Instead, he's having a conversation with someone on his end of the phone. And then I hear what sounds like the phone dropping and then the line goes dead.

I look up to see Ellen in the doorway. She'd been listening all along.

"Lemme guess. He's not coming."

I shake my head. "He said he could do next weekend."

"You know we can't do that. We have to help Mom. You're going to have to call him back."

I hold my stomach like I'm going to be sick. Coulda been the Ben and Jerry's. Probably something else.

Ellen adds, "Look at the bright side. Now you don't have to tell Mom."

CHAPTER ELEVEN

Wooden Barrels

I'M READING IN bed when Ellen knocks on my bedroom door. "Can I come in?" she asks. She opens the door and walks in before I can answer. She's carrying a paper grocery bag close to her side.

"What do you want?"

"I came to see how you were doing. I was a little hard on you earlier."

"You think?"

"If it makes you feel any better, I'm a little bummed out myself."

"Where've you been?"

"Michelle's. Her parents aren't the most available types, either."

"Gina's mom has cancer."

"No kidding. Why didn't you tell me?"

I shrug, and continue reading. I hear Ellen rifling through her grocery bag. She pulls out a can of beer.

"Tah dah!" she says.

"Where'd you get that?"

I close my book and put it on the nightstand next to the framed photo of my dad and me.

"I thought you could use one." She fingers the tab on top and cracks it back. "Here, try it." She hands it to me before reaching for her own.

I sit up in my bed. I take the can and hold it in front of me. I hear the bubbles fizzing inside, and it smells like the old wooden barrel we have on the side of our property from years gone by. The can is cold and slippery in my hand.

"Don't study it—drink it, stupid!" Ellen stares at me like I'm some kind of science project, and I'm not performing as expected.

"Don't rush me!"

Ellen takes a drink of her beer, but keeps a keen eye on me.

I put the can to my lips and tilt it just a bit. The

bubbles break on my lips and they taste like what I imagine is that same wooden barrel we have on the side of our property from years gone by.

"Ew! It tastes like wood."

"Huh," she says. "I never thought of it that way. Try it again."

I decide not to let the taste get in the way of what is destined to be The Moment I First Drank Alcohol. So without thinking, I part my lips, tilt back the can, and take a big, long gulp. It's cold and stale, and strangely dry, as if the whole can was made up of liquid bubbles but if you were to pop them, you would find the can was really only a quarter cup full of the stuff. Light and gassy.

So this is it? Big deal. I take another big swallow and hand the can back to my sister, who smiles, obviously pleased. What a proud moment for her. She pushes the can back in my hands, and then gets another can from the bag.

"Now you got the hang of it." Ellen raises her can in a toast. I raise mine in kind.

"Cheers!" we say in unison.

"Jinx, you owe me a beer," says Ellen.

We don't say another word, but silently drink

from our cans and watch each other, as if this solemn ritual can't be ruined by conversation. I drink the last bit from my can, and then let out a long, loud belch that within seconds has the place reeking. This is the funniest thing that's happened in a long time, and I double up laughing.

"Oh sick! It smells like pizza," Ellen says, which makes me laugh harder, and then she has to try her own burp, and of course it isn't nearly as good or as long or as smelly as mine. I reach in her bag and crack another beer.

"Think you can handle it?"

After I wave her off, she says, "Maybe I misjudged you."

"Can I go with you to Michelle's next time?"

"We'll see."

I feel lighter, better somehow. I gulp the new beer. Strangely enough, this one doesn't taste like wood. It tastes like water. Nice water. My eyes feel good. Happy. I finish off my second beer, and smack the can on top of the nightstand like how I imagine people smack down shot glasses when they're finished with them at a bar. Maybe this is what Gina felt on the labyrinth. I certainly have that calm feeling thingie she was describing.

Now *that's* weird. Ellen and the room are starting to move as if we're on a boat. I didn't know Oregon had earthquakes.

Ellen says in a muffled voice, "You sure you're okay?"

I just laugh and fumble through the grocery bag for the next one. Ellen puts a hand to it.

"Take it easy, Lindsay Lohan."

For some reason this absolutely CRACKS. ME. UP. I sit back on the bed and go into a gut wrenching fit of hysterics.

"Stop! I say, "You're making me sick."

As soon as the words leave my mouth, so does dinner from a few hours ago over the side of my bed. Ellen jumps out of the way just in time.

Ellen yells, "Oh sick! You lightweight."

After I throw up, I roll back and lay on my bed. I break out in a sweat and all I can smell is the stench of my own puke. Wisps of hair are plastered against the side of my head. The underside of my canopy starts to spin and then I see Ellen looking down, glaring at me.

"If you tell, I'll kill you. Got it, creep?"

I nod helplessly, and then the room fades away.

☙

I'M AWAKENED BY Ellen slapping my arm. Somehow I've managed to sit on the side of my bed.

"Clean it up with this," she says, handing me the cleaning supplies. "Throw all the rags in the trash bag and get rid of it."

"You need to help me."

Ellen spits back, "I'm not cleaning this up, Bitsy. You are. And you better do it quick before mom comes home."

She turns on her heels and leaves my room, slamming the door behind her.

I manage to roll over and slide down my bed, carefully avoiding the area where I threw up the inside-out version of my Take-n-Bake pizza. I grab the rags and bucket and get started. It is absolutely disgusting and I wish Ellen had also brought rubber gloves, but I feel too sick to get them for myself. Instead I spend a ton of time scrubbing my hands when I am finished.

After I start a load of laundry and deposit the evidence in the outside trash, I walk through the garage to the backyard and stop at the mouth of the labyrinth. I stare at the brick path in front of me. It's close to ten at night, but pieces of daylight remain. The rain has stopped. It feels like it could start again at any moment. I hear a few night creatures chirping, and a soft breeze makes our quaking Aspens do a little background music.

Why don't I feel you, God? Why does everyone get something out of this labyrinth, but not me?

Nothing happens. I don't expect otherwise. But I just wish for once I had more than a one-sided conversation with God. Everyone else seems to feel something, have questions answered, and be comforted somehow.

And then, something happens. Slowly at first, but then it grows in intensity. I have to hold my hands to my ears. In that quiet, solemn moment in my backyard, at the mouth of the labyrinth, I develop my first hangover-related headache.

CHAPTER TWELVE

Throwing Josie under the Bus

I'M STRAIGHTENING MY hair with a flat iron when my mom enters my bedroom.

"Oh good, you're awake," she says.

I continue to work on my hair. "Thanks for the great time last night, Mother."

"I am so sorry. It's just that it's a very difficult time in Susan's life right now."

"Whatever."

"Ellen told me about Gina's mom."

I flash back to yesterday afternoon, when Gina was lying right here in this room, telling me about her mom.

"I think she's going to die," I say softly.

My mom nods quietly, and then folds her hands

together. "Maybe we should say a prayer for Mrs. Gallagher."

I put down the iron, fold my hands together, and we both close our eyes.

"Lord, I thank You for blessing my family and for keeping my daughters safe. I ask that You comfort the Gallagher Family and help them to know Your plan for them."

I tense up when she says 'Your plan.' I picture God striking people dead at random, just for the fun of it. Like some freaky amusement park game where we're all Whack-a-Moles, and God's holding a big mallet. Where's the plan in that? I let out a loud, sarcastic groan and steal a glance at my mom, who eyes me, disapprovingly. Whatever.

"And please help Gina find You in this time of need. And let Bitsy be a source of strength to Gina during this difficult time."

Here we go again. It's all about serving You, right, God? I let out an impatient sigh, and get ready for the close. I can always tell when my mom is about to finish a prayer.

She looks at me out of the corner of one eye, and says, "And, Lord, in the future, please help

Bitsy find You instead of alcohol. That is always my wish for my girls. In Jesus' name, Amen."

I have been flimflammed!

"Amen," I say, sheepishly. "How did you find out?"

"The garage smells like a bar bathroom at 2:00 a.m. You didn't bother to cover the trash bin last night."

"Why do you assume it was me?"

"Who else is there? Ellen was at Michelle's." She straightens. "I'd really like to know how you managed to get beer at your age."

I open my mouth to say that Ellen is the big, fat reason why I got the beer, but then a vision flashes before my eyes: It's Ellen standing over me as I lay on my spinning bed. She says in a slo-mo demon voice, *If you tell, I'll kill you. Got it, creep?*

"Bitsy?"

"Yeah?"

"I asked you a question."

She waits, expectantly. I say the only logical thing I can think of on a moment's notice.

"It was Josie."

"Josie?!"

"Yeah, Josie gave it to me. She walked right up to her refrigerator and she took it! Just like that. Oh, and she got cigarettes out of the freezer. She smokes too! Did you know that?"

I wait to see if my mom buys this ball of yarn. When she hesitates, I add, "She snuck out a couple of beers, that's all. No biggie."

"Are you smoking?"

"Oh, gross! No way. I swear to God, Mom. No."

"I'm not sure I want you to see Josie anymore."

With muted enthusiasm, I say, "Really? That seems like a fair consequence."

My mom sighs and walks over to the window. With her arms crossed, she stares out the window and I can tell that whatever she's viewing, it's not outside.

"I was your age when I took my first drink. Tried to fill that hole inside. Didn't work, of course."

I think about last night. For the brief few minutes before I got sick, I felt pretty good. Pretty flippin' great, actually.

She doesn't look at me, but continues to stare

out the window. "I wish I could save you years of grief finding this out for yourself, but the simple act of helping others will make you happier than you've ever dreamed. So happy you won't need to take a drink to make peace with the world."

I bristle. "One of God's mighty soldiers, right?"

"That's why I help people like Susan stop drinking. It's the only way I know to stay sober. And be happy."

"Can we speed things up a little? I don't want to waste one more minute when we could be out saving the world."

My mom starts to react but reconsiders. Instead, she says calmly, "I'm going to pray for you. If it doesn't change you, it'll at least help me."

"This God of yours has you wrapped around His little finger, you know that? Instead of prayers, why don't you do something productive? Let's start with making dinner. There's some good service work for you." I lean back in my chair and stare defiantly at my mother.

She looks stunned. Seeing my words have found a home, I drive it. "I would think being with your kids is a good enough reason to be peaceful and happy. Otherwise, who really cares if you drink yourself to death?!"

"Bitsy!"

The phone rings like a bell going off at the end of a round. My sister Ellen yells upstairs, "Mom? Phone."

Dripping with sarcasm, I say, "*Of course* it's for you."

My mom moves toward the door. Before she leaves, she commands, "You're grounded for the entire weekend! No TV, no computer, no music, no cell phone, no friends. If I catch you drinking again I will take those things out back, build a bon fire, and burn them, that clear?!"

We have a stand-off with our eyes.

I say in a measured tone, "You're going to burn my friends?"

"You better watch it."

Ellen calls up again, "Mom?"

My mom straightens and leaves the room. I exhale for what seems like the first time all morning.

Are you there, God? It's me, Bitsy. Hey, thanks a lot. Most kids get away with having their first beer, but not me. Why couldn't you have given me a clueless mom, or even a Rock Star mom, like the ones on Behind the Scenes Videos?

I am quickly reminded that things could be a lot worse. I could have Gina's mom, and then soon I might not have any mom at all. I consider saying another prayer to God, just to thank Him for the guilt trip, but instead I brush my teeth an extra long time since each one feels like it's wrapped inside a baby mitten. I guzzle five Dixie cups full of cold water, and then trudge downstairs to the kitchen. I still feel a little queasy from last night. Give me a break! It was only two stupid beers! Ellen is right; I am a lightweight. And I almost feel bad for throwing Josie under the bus like that, but what else could I do?

CHAPTER THIRTEEN

Exotic Mrs. Gallagher

THE SUN BURNS bright in the clear blue sky as I sit on my porch, looking for my friends on the Yellow Brick Road. I check my phone: NO MESSAGES. I text my dad: CAN I LIVE WITH U??? I hold out my phone to take a picture of myself. After three tries, I get one that looks pretty good and I send that to my dad as well. Maybe when he gets here he can talk to my mom about letting me visit more often. Maybe when I visit I can turn the visit into a long stay. Maybe . . .

I'm startled to see Mrs. Gallagher's SUV pull into my driveway.

"Hurry, my mom's late for an appointment," Gina calls out her window.

I waste no time and run down the driveway. Before I can jump in the car, Mrs. Gallagher has her window down, and she asks, "Is your mother home?"

I freeze.

"No. She had to be somewhere."

Mrs. Gallagher's lips purse together in disapproval. "You're alone? Should you lock the front door?"

"Uh, no. Ellen's here."

This seems to satisfy her. I jump in the backseat and feel a stab of guilt when I see Josie sitting back there as well. So I do what anyone would do. I ignore her.

Mrs. Gallagher backs out of the driveway and slowly my heart returns to its normal rhythm. The car is a little warm yet I notice Mrs. Gallagher is wearing a long-sleeved blouse. I also notice her cheekbones seem larger than normal which is a weird thing to notice. She looks almost exotic from her profile. And then I feel bad because I realize it must mean she's losing more weight.

As soon as Mrs. Gallagher and Gina start talking, I hold up my phone to Josie and mouth the words: "Why didn't anyone text me we were getting a ride?"

"Dude, look again," says Josie.

I check my phone. A text message is now waiting, obviously sent as they were pulling in. I scowl at Josie who looks pleased with herself.

Gina asks me over the front seat, "How did it go with your dad?"

I see Mrs. Gallagher's eyes dart to meet mine in the rearview mirror.

"He, uh, couldn't make it."

Josie asks, "What happened?"

Everyone's watching me, waiting for the scoop. I am saved by yet another accessory: "Josie! You got new glasses," I say, admiring her chunky teal frames.

She instinctively puts her hand up to her face and nudges them higher on her nose. "Oh, these? I got them over the weekend at the coast. Like 'em?"

"Love them!" I say, and the conversation moves to how great Josie's face looks.

As they're talking, I'm daydreaming. Being grounded for the weekend wasn't so bad. Josie was gone anyway. Gina didn't want to leave her mom's side. Ellen stayed in her room. The only one I really missed seeing was Nick. And my dad, of course.

Only four more days 'til the big lavender festival, and I am completely psyched. My mom's been working in the fields nonstop, and I helped her all weekend bundling lavender and making sachets with lavender seeds. She was pretty self-absorbed and seemed to forget about the drinking incident, which oddly enough kinda bummed me out.

Mrs. Gallagher says to me, "Is your mother getting ready for the festival, dear?"

"Yeah. She's nervous about the heat wave. They said it's supposed to last all week."

"I told my husband I'd like to go this year," she says, gripping her leather covered steering wheel. "I've lived here my entire life and I've never managed to visit a lavender farm. I heard the festival's a lovely event."

"It's pretty cool," I offer.

"Will she make her labyrinth available to the public?"

"Yeah, I suppose. I mean, it's always open as far as I know."

She appears to be thinking something over but doesn't say another word. We reach the park entrance and say our thank-yous as Mrs. Gallagher drops us off in the street.

To me she says, "Now make sure to tell your mother I said hello." I just smile.

Right, like *that's* going to happen.

She says to Gina, "I should be home after lunch. Love you, sweetheart."

"Love you too," Gina replies, and I have to look away because I swear I see Mrs. Gallagher's eyes get watery.

I walk toward the kids' play area, but my friends stay in the street until the SUV rounds the corner, and then they start walking down the Yellow Brick Road. Now I'm irritated. "Hey! I'm not going back to Dylan's," I say, "You can just forget it, Gina."

"Don't worry. C'mon," she says.

"Where we going?" I ask.

Gina and Josie exchange a knowing look. Josie lights a cigarette.

CHAPTER FOURTEEN

The Caretaker

WE WALK IN silence for awhile and then Gina says, "Just a bit farther now."

I look ahead. On our left is a small church with a large sign in front that reads NOW ENROLL-ING FOR FALL PRESCHOOL. INQUIRE WITHIN. On the other side of the church is the funeral home and cemetery. After that, a Starbucks.

"I didn't bring any money for iced lattes," I say. I wished I had, though, because it's freakin' hot and I'm thirsty.

"We're not going there."

Before I can ask another question, Gina walks past the wrought iron gate and into the cemetery.

"Aha, the Zone. Are Nick and Dylan coming?" I ask.

Josie looks at me like I belong in the preschool next door. I point to the funeral home, and say, "I wonder if their business is dead. Get it? Cuz of the cemetery?"

They just stare at me, stone-faced. It made me laugh, anyway.

Josie snaps at me, "Grow up!" Then to Gina, she says, "Are you okay?"

I close my eyes, realizing my stupid mistake. Gina ignores us both, and veers into the cemetery driveway.

After much searching, we arrive at the place Gina wants us to see. We all take swigs from our water bottles and read a headstone with the words:

RITA BROWN
BORN FEB 19, 1958 – DIED MAR 4, 1985

"What is it?" I am thoroughly confused.

"Sorry, Bits," says Gina, "I didn't want to freak you out."

Josie walks away and pretends to read nearby headstones. What is going on here?

"I know you've had a bad week," I say, "but you're seriously starting to scare me. Can you please tell me what's going on?"

Gina looks so pale that I wonder if she has seen the ghost of Rita Brown, Resident Dead Person. Finally she says, "Thanks for letting me walk your labyrinth last week."

"I'm glad it helped."

"When I got home, I felt calm enough to ask my mom more questions. You know, questions I was kinda afraid to ask before."

"Such as . . . "

"Like, how bad is it, are you going to die, when are you going to die, that sort of thing."

We both look far beyond the gravestones to an open area with rolling hills and green grass. The Caretaker we ran from before now wears overalls and sits on a riding lawn mower. When he spots us, he waves. We turn to make sure he's waving at us and not someone else. We wave back when we realize it's for us.

"No one can know when they'll die, not even your mom."

"No, but they have a pretty good idea. Especially since it's spread all over."

I don't want to ask, but I hear myself saying, "So, she's going to die?"

Gina looks at the headstone again. "This is where my mom's family is buried. This is my mom's sister, my aunt Rita."

I close my eyes. I just called Gina's aunt a Resident Dead Person. "I'm sorry."

"I didn't know her. She died before I was born."

I scan the headstone and the surrounding area. A row behind it sits two more, close together, both with the name BROWN written on them. Next to them, another light gray stone rests but there's no inscription.

Gina says, "That one over there will say Gallagher."

I bow my head and walk over to the blank stone. So this is where Gina's mom will be buried.

Josie has returned. While they talk, I walk around the blank headstone so my back is to my friends. *Hey God, what's up with this?!* I clasp my hands tighter and squeeze my eyes shut as hard as possible, as if these gestures might get me a better connection to The Great Almighty. *Why do You have to take Gina's mom? What about all the murder-*

*ers and rapists and child molesters out there? She's just
a Realtor, for God's Sake!*

I feel a stab of guilt. One, because I just took
the Lord's name in vain, and, two, because I bet
all of the murderers, rapists, and child molesters
have people saying prayers for them, too, and here
I am wishing death upon them.

*Why do You have to make it so hard on every-
body? Gina should be at the park right now, not in a
cemetery.*

I hear someone approaching, so I quickly close,
Please help, Amen.

"Greetings, girls!"

It's the Caretaker on the riding lawn mower,
only now he's parked it along the road and is walking toward us. Now that he's standing, I can see
he's rather short, no taller than me. Josie crushes
out her cigarette on the bottom of her shoe as I
make my way back to my friends. The Caretaker
and I reach them at the same time.

"Hi," we say in unison. As he approaches I
notice that his wrinkles look like they are cut into
his face, mostly around his eyes. Those are a deep
brown, and for some reason they remind me of

our dog, Chip, who stayed in California with my dad.

"We weren't doing anything wrong," Josie says, pointing to Aunt Rita's headstone. "We have as much right to be here as she does!"

"What can I do you for today?" he says with a wide grin.

I'm guessing dentures. Those teeth are too straight and white to be the real thing.

"We're here for my family," says Gina.

The Caretaker surveys the stones, and then says, "Are you the Gallagher girl?"

"How did you know?"

He pulls his cap off and scratches his head. "I make it my business to know everyone. Why I remember when your folks moved into their home, what, ten years past. You were just a baby then."

Gina straightens. "I would've been a least three!"

He chuckles. "Of course you were." He tucks his hat back on and says, "I'm sorry to hear about your mother. She came by th' other day. Told me all about it, she did." He nods toward Aunt Rita, Resident Dead Person.

Gina wraps her arms around herself and sways a bit. I move forward and answer for her, "Thank you," I say. I can tell she's about to cry but is doing her best to keep it together.

"You girls want somethin' to drink? There's a fridge full of pop in the buildin'." He points his thumb to the back of the cemetery.

"YES!" We cry. I can't wait to get my hands on a cold one since it's another scorcher and my feet are practically sliding out of my flip flops.

"Well, c'mon then!" he says, waving us over.

I've gotta give it to him. He's zippy for an old dude. We're practically jogging to keep up with him. The 'buildin'' he's referring to is actually the funeral home. We get to the back door and the first things I notice are stand up metal ashtrays. People must smoke a lot at these events.

He hesitates at the door. "I can bring 'em out, or you can drink 'em inside, it's up to you."

I peer through the windows and spot some cushy chairs arranged at the end of the hall. They look comfortable and inviting. Before I can say anything, Gina says, "We'd like to come inside, thanks."

He smiles and pulls open the door. We're met with a welcome blast of air conditioning. As he steps inside, it occurs to me for the first time that maybe this guy isn't so nice. Like maybe he has three of his crony friends waiting in the back and once we go inside they'll all jump us and do horrible things, and then we'll end up in one of those caskets. I tug Gina back and whisper, "Hey! Is this safe? What if he's a serial killer? Let's send Josie first."

Gina smirks at me. "Will you relax? He works with the dead. He doesn't make them that way."

It turns out I have nothing to fear. The back door leads to an open area with rooms on both sides, each with glass walls so you can look inside. The Caretaker acts as a tour guide, stopping at each door so he can tell us about the room and so we can take a good look. Three of the rooms are used for funeral services. The fourth is a chapel that has an altar, a jumbo cross, and pews.

As we peer into the chapel, he says quietly, "Life ain't easy. No doubt about it. I've seen my share a troubles. Why, I didn't know how I'd ever laugh again after my wife died. But, rest assured, it happens."

We move on. One of the three funeral rooms has a casket, along with dozens of waist-high flower arrangements. He nods toward its door. It has a slide-in card on the front that reads: HAR-RISON. The card thing is a good idea. Other-wise, with a closed casket, how would you know who's who? Especially during flu season when it's bound to get crowded.

"Meningitis," he says as if to answer our unspoken question. "Left behind a wife, three kids, and two grandbabies." He shakes his head. "My mother always said it's written on your forehead. When you pass, that is."

Josie presses her hand to her forehead and inspects her palm for clues.

We all peer inside the window to get a better look at the casket. When he sees this, he adds, "I shouldn't a put stories in your head. Comes with the job, I guess."

We reach the other end of the building. "Pop's in the fridge," he says, nodding to an office door.

Tucked on the other side of the office is an alcove with couches, Formica tables, plastic chairs and a small kitchen area.

We all gather near the office and he opens his

personal fridge, saying, "Let's see . . . I have Black Cherry, Cream Soda, Rock & Rye, and Redpop."

Josie exclaims, "You have Faygo? I love Faygo! My parents are from Michigan!" She manically jumps in front of everyone.

I quietly chime to Gina, "Cuckoo clock."

Josie giggles, "I'll have a Redpop, please. How did you get it here?"

The Caretaker chuckles, "I have my ways."

I choose Cream Soda and Gina takes Black Cherry. He lets us sit in those comfy chairs and relax a bit in the air conditioning while he works in his office. When we peek our heads around the office door to say thanks, he jumps up from his desk and walks us back outside.

On the way to the graves, he grabs some work gloves and a pail from the riding lawn mower.

"Thanks again," I say.

"It was my pleasure. I'm glad you could make it."

Did we have an appointment? I wonder. I make a mental note to ask Gina about this later.

Gina asks, "Maybe we could come back sometime?"

"Absolutely! You're always welcome."

The Caretaker regards Gina as he wriggles his hands into the dirty, stiff work gloves.

"You need to know that no one knows the 'why' a things. It's just s'posed to be. And I hope one day you'll understand not the 'why,' but the 'how' of it. How you can find peace, that is."

I don't have the foggiest idea what he's just said, but it sounds good, and for the first time in days, *I* feel good. I can tell Gina and Josie feel the same way because we all have goofy smiles plastered on our faces.

The Caretaker returns the smile and I get this wicked thought to ask him if those teeth were bought and paid for, but I restrain myself.

"Peace be with you, girls," he says, and then he picks up the pail and turns to leave. "I've got a date with the weeds. Persistent little buggers."

CHAPTER FIFTEEN

Truth or Dunk

AFTER OUR CEMETERY excursion, we all go back to the park since this was the original plan. It has to be at least ninety degrees again. My mom worries about the heat and how it will affect her lavender field. We hope the weather breaks in time for the festival. Who wants to hang out in a hot barn in the sweltering heat, even if it is nicely decorated and you can have all the lavender lemonade you want?

We walk over to a shaded, grassy area and plop down for a rest, and I'm bummed to see the crowd at the fountain. Gina and I swap looks.

I offer, "I guess it's not too bad."

"Dude, are you clueless?" snaps Josie. "It looks like the whole school's here!"

"I don't want to go over there, guys," says Gina. "They'll just ask questions about my mom. I'm not ready for that."

"What about your pool?" I ask.

"I'm not sure my mom would want people over."

Josie lays into me. "What were you thinking?"

Gina looks like she's considering something, and then says, "On the other hand, my mom doesn't want us to act differently just because she's sick."

I grin triumphantly at Josie. Ha!

Gina chews her lip and watches the kids mill around the park. "C'mon, let's go to my house!"

Dylan and Nick are just walking up as Gina finishes. Dylan tosses a football in the air. "Sounds good!" he says, as if he should naturally be included.

Gina laughs and says, "Fine. You too, Nick."

My stomach flips and I turn to hide my smile.

Twenty minutes later, Josie and I are doing cannonballs off the side of the pool. I watch Gina flirt with Dylan, and I have a new appreciation for him. If Dylan can make Gina smile at this time in her life, then he's okay in my book.

I come up for air from my latest cannonball, and Nick is directly in front of me. "Oh!" I say, "You scared me."

Nick whispers in my ear, "Heard you were grounded over the weekend, but no one's talking. What happened?"

"Oh, that. I acted *disrespectfully* toward my mom. Her words." I laugh for good measure when I say this last part. This will be my official stock answer. I've decided I don't want my friends to know that I can't keep down a couple of beers.

"You? Disrespectful? Isn't that Ellen's job?"

"She took the day off, what can I say?" I look through the water at my distorted feet, treading water. I feel like I'm lying, but I'm really only omitting certain things.

"Uh, hello? This is Nick. What are you keeping from me?"

"Nothing."

"Tell me or I'll dunk you."

"Very funny."

"I mean it."

"You wouldn't dare." I swim away from Nick, but he swims faster and cuts me off.

"Last chance, Bits. Fess up." He puts his hands on my shoulders and I brace myself for the plunge.

"Ahem!"

We both look up and, sure enough, Mrs. Gallagher stands at the side of the pool; her hand pats the side of her head. She's no longer wearing her business outfit. Now she's in sweats and a sweatshirt, despite the hot weather. She eyes us like we've just been caught shoplifting.

Nick drops his hands in the water with a splash and I swim toward the side of the pool. He quickly swims in the opposite direction. Mrs. Gallagher doesn't take her eyes off Nick until he's out of the water and rummaging through the pool toys near the side of the pool. Dylan jumps out to help him.

I overhear Dylan say quietly to Nick, "Dude, she's got you totally locked on radar. Happened to me last year, before she got to know me."

Nick sizes up Dylan, and responds, "And you're still here."

Dylan just smiles proudly.

Gina is my loyal friend in need, because she quickly declares that a game of Marco Polo is in order. Josie fights with her over who should be "it" first. My back's to the side of the pool with my arms resting on the lip while my body floats up in front of me. I notice Mrs. Gallagher's now staring *me* down, so I offer up a smile and a shrug, just so she's aware that I wasn't the one who started it with Nick.

"Bitsy," she says, "May I please speak to you?"

"Sure."

"Can you come out of the pool?"

"Marco!" Gina yells. With her eyes squeezed shut, she jumps toward Josie, who yells, "Polo!" and manages to dive under the water and away from Gina just in time.

Mrs. Gallagher takes a step back from the pool to avoid the splashes. "Bitsy?" she says.

"Sure, I'm coming," I say. I take my time getting out of the pool. I have this weird sensation that I am being watched by both Mrs. Gallagher and Nick, and it makes me feel hyper-self conscious. Get a grip! It's not like my bathing suit's going to spontaneously burst into flames or anything.

Mrs. Gallagher says to Gina, "Honey, I'll just be a minute with Bitsy," and then waits expectantly for me to grab my towel and dry off.

"Let's go inside," she says.

Oh no.

CHAPTER SIXTEEN

An Invitation

I QUICKLY BRUSH the water from me and wrap the towel around my waist.

Mrs. Gallagher palms the side of her head again and I notice for the first time that her hairspray isn't as crispy today. As a matter of fact, I'm not so sure she's even wearing any!

I reluctantly follow her inside. Mrs. Gallagher sits at the kitchen table, but I remain standing. Even though their air conditioning's turned down because Mrs. Gallagher gets cold easily, I'm shivering like crazy. We just look at each other: Mrs. Gallagher at the table and me at the sliding glass door.

I finally stammer, "Nick is *so* annoying."

She chuckles. "That's not what this is about."

I breathe a sigh of relief.

"I know you and Gina are best friends."

I shift my weight from one foot to the other. "Yeah."

"And I must admit I haven't always been comfortable with it, what with your mom being a free spirit and all." Mrs. Gallagher takes a Kleenex from the box next to her, and twists it into a small tissue rope between her fingers. "But that was a long time ago, before I got to know you." She nods at the window. "She said she walked your labyrinth last week."

"It seemed like it really helped her."

"I normally wouldn't approve of something so unorthodox, but . . . "

Mrs. Gallagher's words trail off and she looks at me as if waiting for a response.

"My mom wouldn't use it if it was bad. You thought you were a Jesus freak? Believe me, my mom's right up there with you."

Mrs. Gallagher looks amused. Suddenly, it occurs to me. "Maybe *you* should try it!"

"Me?!" she says, and I can't tell if she's surprised by that idea or not.

"Seriously, why not? You've got nothing to lose, and it did help Gina."

"Maybe during the festival."

"Why wait? My mom's not going to care."

She seems to consider the offer.

I look through the window and see the others playing in the pool. Josie's laughing and splashing water at Nick. Hmmm.

"Look," I say. "I kinda have to go. Did you need me for anything else?"

She smiles weakly at me. "I just wanted to say thank you for being such a good friend to my Gina. She's going to need . . . your support this year."

I clear my throat. Yet another pregnant pause. And then I say it. The most idiotic, embarrassing thing I could possibly say.

"I really liked your headstone, Mrs. Gallagher."

Mrs. Gallagher stops twisting the Kleenex and stares at me. "What did you say?"

I feel my foot stepping into that camouflaged rope trap once again.

"I, uh, like your headstone. Gina showed me."

Mrs. Gallagher cries, "I thought you were at the park!"

"Oh! We were there, too, but it was crowded."

I'm stepping in it, I'm definitely stepping in it.

She blows her nose. "I think I will take you up on your offer."

"You will?" I didn't see this one coming.

"I'll stop by later today."

OMG!

"Great!" I say, "My mom's going to love it!"

Mrs. Gallagher brightens, as if a burden's been lifted. I raise my fist proudly. "Rock on, Mrs. G!"

"I don't know what that means, but thank you."

Pleased, I start to leave.

"And Bitsy? Be careful, dear. About Nick."

"Whahaat?"

"I see how he looks at you. I know you've been friends for a very long time, but you girls are getting to an age where you'll see that look more and more. Trust me, dear."

She smiles and pats the side of her head. I walk quickly and exit through the sliding glass door before she can say another word.

Once outside, I lean against the door as if I just made it out of North Korea. I scan the pool. Nick is "it" in the Marco Polo game. I smile. Josie moves directly in front of him and gets tagged in an obvious play to get touched by him.

"Oh! You got me!" Josie says, giggling.

Nick opens his eyes in surprise. My eyes narrow on Josie, the Traitor.

Gina notices me and quickly jumps out of the pool. "Keep playing," she says to the others.

"What did she say?" she asks.

"She asked about our labyrinth. Wants to try it. Apparently your good review made her curious."

"Wow. I never thought I would see that happen."

"Yeah, and you never told her we went to the cemetery, either."

"How did she know that?"

"Uh, well, I, you know, it came up in conversation."

Gina grabs my hand. "Is she mad?"

"No! No. She's not mad. Just surprised, I think, that's all." How do I tell Gina that her mom cried her eyes out when she found out that her daughter visited her Resident Dead Sister and her unmarked grave?

"Where are you going?" Gina asks me as I gather up my stuff.

"I need to get back to my mom. I promised her I'd help in the fields. Lavender festival this weekend." I look past Gina and see Nick watching me. When he sees me, he smiles. I wave goodbye and he frowns. And then, Josie tags him.

"Ha!" she shouts triumphantly.

I want to kill her.

"Bye, guys!" I yell to everyone.

Gina gives me a big hug, and I don't even mind that she's soaking wet and I have to towel off again before changing my clothes. I quickly walk home, thinking about Nick and how Mrs. Gallagher is right about him. We've been friends for four years and this is the first time I've ever wanted to kiss him. What's up with that?

CHAPTER SEVENTEEN

Walk of Independence

MY MOM'S IN the fields, cutting and bundling lavender.

"Where's Ellen?" I ask.

"She went to a movie."

"I thought she was going to help us."

"She's going to help by making dinner tonight. I have to run . . . "

"Yeah, yeah, I know. The lady needs me, blah-bity, blah."

"What has gotten into you?"

"Nothing. I'll go grab my stuff."

I find my shears and gloves in the shed, and head back toward the fields. When I get there, I tell my mom point-blank, "Mrs. Gallagher's coming by today."

"Is that so? Are you in trouble? "

"No, but thanks for automatically going there."

"I wonder if she wants some lavender. It is medicinal."

"Brace yourself," I say proudly. "She wants to walk our labyrinth."

My mom puts down her tools. Sweat drips off her face. "She's coming to walk . . . our labyrinth?"

"You heard it correctly. And I made it happen."

My mom shakes her head and smiles. "I never thought I'd see the day."

"What is it about you two, anyway?"

"Two things. One, I'm a drunk, and, two, I'm a *dee-vorce-ay.*"

"The entire world's divorced. You say it like it's a dirty word."

"To Jean Gallagher, it is."

"She's not so bad. A little strict, maybe." I think about her noticing Nick, and I can't help but smile.

"Not to be confused with rigid. Or narrow minded."

"You sound chapped."

My mom looks at her fields and considers this. I continue to cut lavender stalks next to her.

"You know, you're right. And I really can't afford a resentment right now. I guess I just don't like to be judged."

"And you're not a drunk. You haven't been a drunk in over four years."

She laughs. "You don't need to drink to be a drunk."

"You know what I mean."

"I do." My mom takes her sheers and clips a few stalks. "So how is she doing anyway?"

"Okay, I guess. Although I'm fairly confident she didn't use hairspray today."

My mom laughs. "That's impossible!"

"I saw it with my own two eyes!" It feels good to laugh with my mom, even if it is at someone else's expense. I add, "Gina showed me her mom's gravestone today."

"That's a little morbid."

"I kinda liked it."

"And you thought I was weird?"

"I don't think you're weird, Mom."

"What about the labyrinth?"

I shrug. "It's okay."

"Ellen said you wished it was a swimming pool."

"She's such a big mouth!"

"It's okay. It's not as if I didn't know you felt that way."

I continue to cut stalks. "Want me to get the wheelbarrow and take these in?"

"That'd be great."

I stand up and swish away a few bumbles. I start toward the shed when I see Mrs. Gallagher open the back gate and tiptoe through the rocky path on the side of our garage. Her hair looks like it's been sprayed since I last saw her. "Hello?" she calls.

I wave to her.

"Why, Jean," My mom calls back, wiping her hands on the side of her pants. "How nice of you to drop by." She goes to greet Mrs. Gallagher.

I relax and turn my attention to the fields. When they begin to walk together toward the labyrinth, I find a wheelbarrow from the shed and bring it to the lavender, where I gather and bundle loose stalks for drying. Every now and then I look to see my mom and Mrs. Gallagher's progress. They spend a lot of time at the mouth of the labyrinth. I decide to get my two cents in to God before Mrs. Gallagher grabs His attention.

God, it's me, Bitsy. I hope you can hear me. Please walk the labyrinth with Mrs. Gallagher, would You? She needs something right now. Thank you that my mom can help Mrs. Gallagher when she needs it.

I stop for a minute to consider if I really am thankful that my mom is helping one more person.

I look up and see that my mom is walking next to Mrs. Gallagher on the labyrinth, her hands clasped together, and I'm struck by the "worlds colliding" moment: my mom in her work shorts, U of O baseball cap and loafers, and Mrs. Gallagher in her matching pantsuit, hairsprayed hair, and chunky high heels.

I feel like a peeping Tom but can't help myself. They walk to the center of the labyrinth, stop for a few minutes, and then Mrs. Gallagher takes the lead and they slowly walk back to the entrance. When they're finished, they talk a few minutes longer, and then the unexpected happens. Mrs. Gallagher hugs my mom tightly. My mom returns the hug and they don't let go right away. When they do, Mrs. Gallagher pushes her hair in place and my mom wipes her hands again on her pants. They talk some more and then they look at me.

Busted! I immediately look away and pretend like I've been cutting lavender the whole time. When I steal a look out of the corner of my eye, Mrs. Gallagher is already nearing the back gate, and my mom's calling out, "See you tomorrow!"

Mrs. Gallagher waves goodbye. Tomorrow?

After she's gone, I drop my tools and run toward the labyrinth. When I reach my mom, she laughs and holds up a hand before I can say anything. "No questions," she says. When she sees I really need something, anything, she adds, "We had a nice time, and I invited her to walk the labyrinth again whenever she'd like, so she said she'd like to come back in the morning."

"You're kidding."

"No, I think it really helped her."

"That's great."

She pulls off her cap and wipes her hairline with the back of her hand. "It must be a hundred. This better break soon." She looks at me a long moment, then asks, "Would you like some lemonade? I'm parched."

"Sure. I'll be there in a minute." I watch her walk into the kitchen before I turn to face the labyrinth.

Walk of Independence

You pulled a fast one, didn't you? I don't know what happened, but it's nice to see my mom and Gina's mom together, God.

I walk to the entrance of the labyrinth. I look down at the swirling path in front of me. Beyond, I see the lavender fields and the wheelbarrow at its rim. All is quiet, except for the buzzing of a few random bees. I find it hard to imagine that in just a few days this place will be swarming with people, listening to music on outdoor speakers, taking photographs in the lavender fields, and purchasing art from vendors. The Lavender Festival has become the event of the summer, according to the mayor, and every year people show up from all over to attend.

I put my left foot on the path's entrance and retract it, like a swimmer testing the waters. Ironic, since I have wished all along that this labyrinth was a swimming pool. I try again, and this time I slowly move forward, one foot in front of the other. I take a deep breath and exhale. I notice a hairline crack in one of the pavers. Toward the inside right of the path, I spot a few tiny weeds growing up through the gaps. What was it the Caretaker said about the weeds? *Persistent little buggers.* The outermost ring of the labyrinth is still wet from the sprinkler's overspray. I feel like I am walking the path in "real time," instead of trying to get through it so I can move on with my day.

I don't want to need You, God. My mom's needed you, and then she's had to spend the rest of her life doing Your will. I don't want to be Your slave. Why go after the humans anyway? Don't you have an army of angels at your beck and call? I'm sorry I feel that way, but there you go. I do appreciate you comforting Gina, and making Mrs. Gallagher and my mom talk. I'm also grateful when you keep me from killing Ellen. Just kidding. I would never really do it. You know that, right?

I am officially at the middle of the labyrinth. I stop and take another deep breath. I don't have anything to leave behind.

Thanks for everything. I'll take it from here.

I walk the way I came, the tiny weeds now on the left. I step over the cracked paver, and keep walking until I am off the path.

When I finally make it inside the kitchen, my mom's nowhere to be found, but a full glass of lemonade is on the table. Bittersweet.

CHAPTER EIGHTEEN

Like Mother, Like Daughter

I'M SITTING AT my desk in my room, working on my computer. I pick up my cell phone just in case I missed anything. It reads: NO MESSAGES. My dad has yet to respond to the photo I sent. I start a follow up text to him: ABOUT THE WEEKEND . . . I pause, and stare at the flashing cursor.

I hear a knock on my door and quickly end my unsent text message.

"Can I come in?" asks Ellen. She walks in before I can say anything. "Dinner's ready."

"Thanks, now get outta my room."

"I heard Gina's mom was here. I'm impressed." Ellen plops on my bed. "Whatcha reading?"

I lean over to Ellen and sniff. "It's your trademark perfume. Beer and smokes."

"You're like a drug dog. Down, Fido!"

She wears a glassy-eyed, perma grin. She's buzzed. I decide to drop it.

"It's a site on Hospice. Gina says her mom's going to need it."

"That's some light reading."

"I suppose *National Enquirer* is more your speed."

"You might want to pick up a copy, Bits. You could actually learn something."

"The next two months are going to suck. They say it eats you alive from the inside out."

"Who's this 'they' person? Doctors are wrong all the time. Geez, have a little faith, will you?"

"I do have faith. Faith that she'll be dead by Labor Day."

I instantly regret saying it.

"You're lucky mom isn't around to hear you."

"Mom's never around."

Ellen sizes me up and says, "Oh, so that's it. You're twisted cuz she's not here."

"No, I'm not."

"I think you are. Man, you're selfish."

"Why should I care what you think? You're going to turn out just like her."

Ellen looks baffled, but amused.

"Your drinking?" I say to clarify, "You don't think mom started out this way? I give you a year."

I resume my web search.

"Until what?"

"Why, rehab, of course. And then you'll have to do God's Grand Plan work until the day you die."

Ellen bursts into hysterics, and I have to admit, it sounds pretty ridiculous to me too when I say it out loud.

"Is that what you believe?"

"That you'll be in rehab?"

"No, stupid," she tries to say between fits of laughter, "That mom's running around doing God's . . . Grand Plan . . . work!"

"Why else would she be with that stupid lady right now if she didn't have to?"

Ellen finally pulls it together, which is good, because I'm as close as ever to killing her. She says, "Mom sees that lady because she wants to, not because she has to."

"Shut up."

"Come on." Ellen must sense that I'm at my limit, because she stops laughing and stares at me. I think I detect pity in her eyes, and this makes me even angrier.

"Would you just go?"

She shakes her head like I'm broken beyond repair. "Chicken's in the oven. I'm heading back over to Michelle's."

"Thanks."

She closes the door and I'm finally alone. Again. I think about my mom in the lavender field, telling me she doesn't like to be judged by Mrs. Gallagher. Why shouldn't she judge? My mom can't even keep her own kids under control.

I smack the computer mouse on my desk and try to focus on the monitor screen. Finally, I pick up my phone again and text my dad: I CAN'T W8T 2CU!

CHAPTER NINETEEN

The Unexpected

I DIDN'T HEAR my mom come home last night, which is good, because I think I would've lost it.

After about twenty minutes of reading in bed, considering whether or not to even bother with breakfast, I finally head downstairs. Through the picture window, I spot Mrs. Gallagher's SUV parked in our driveway, right behind my mom's bike. The giant gas guzzler makes the bike look like a kid's toy in comparison. I go through the kitchen and walk outside. My mom and Mrs. Gallagher are sitting on our patio, talking.

"Hey," I say.

Mrs. Gallagher smiles warmly at me. "Why,

hello, Bitsy. Will you be coming by for a swim later? It's going to be another record breaking day."

My mom sees me too and smiles, but I respond with a cold, stony stare. When I'm satisfied she got the message, I turn and say sweetly to Mrs. Gallagher, "Yes, thank you. I told Gina I'd be there at eleven."

"I was just telling your mother how glad I am you talked me into trying the labyrinth." Mrs. Gallagher pats my mom's knee the way she likes to pat the side of her head. My mom smiles in return.

I give my mom a dirty look, and then offer up her stock response, "I'm so glad I could be of service."

My mom eyes me with suspicion.

"About the festival," I say to my mom. "I have to miss Saturday. Dad's coming to visit."

My mom flinches.

Mrs. Gallagher says, "He rescheduled? How nice."

I take a big gulp. Oh, man. I didn't see that one coming.

She continues talking to my mom, "Bitsy was telling us in the car yesterday that her father couldn't make it last weekend."

Mrs. Gallagher's words hang in the air. My gulp turns into a choke.

Mrs. Gallagher smiles warmly at my mom before asking, "Will Bitsy's new stepmother be joining him?"

"I don't know," she says, then turns to me and asks, "Will your new stepmother be joining him, Elizabeth?"

Now it's my mom who has *me* totally locked on radar.

"Uh, no, uh . . . "

My mom continues, "I was just about to offer Jean a glass of lavender tea. Can you get that for me, darling?"

I break away from my mom's gaze and see Mrs. Gallagher smiling at me gratefully. I make a run for the door.

Inside the kitchen, I eavesdrop on my mom and Mrs. Gallagher.

Mrs. Gallagher watches a bee hover over a potted plant nearby. "I heard that lavender honey is heavenly," she says to my mom.

I can tell my mom's barely listening. "You'll have to try some during the festival. We'll have samples."

I grab the tea and head for the kitchen door. I just make it outside when I hear my mom say, "Jean, will you excuse me? I need to check on something."

"Of course. I'll use the labyrinth again, if you don't mind." Mrs. Gallagher stands, smoothes the creases on her pants, and starts toward the labyrinth.

My mom walks toward me. "Help yourself," she says over her shoulder, "I'll keep your tea cold." She meets me at the door.

Mrs. Gallagher walks to the mouth of the labyrinth. She positions herself, takes a deep breath.

My mom says quietly to me, so Mrs. Gallagher can't hear, "What in God's name do you mean, your father's coming to visit?"

I hesitate. "Um, Ellen was supposed to tell you."

"Why didn't *you* tell me?!"

Mrs. Gallagher steps onto the labyrinth.

My mom stares daggers at me and I completely break under the pressure. I speed talk, "He-was-supposed-to-come-last-weekend-when-he-told-CoCo-he-was-going-on-a-golf-trip-only-he-couldn't-make-it-so-he-rescheduled-for-this-weekend."

My mom blinks a few times. "Who the hell is Coco?"

I look down, ashamed. "I meant, Charlene."

"I can't believe this!"

"I tried to tell you . . . "

"Really? Was that before or after you shared the good news with Jean Gallagher?"

Mrs. Gallagher smacks the side of her neck.

"Ouch!" she cries.

My mom and I turn to see Mrs. Gallagher look down and watch something fall near her feet on the labyrinth. "Oh, a bee," she says.

Mrs. Gallagher looks at us as her hand continues to hold the side of her neck. She starts to breathe really hard, like she can't catch her breath. My mom runs to her. I accidentally let the glass of tea slide out of my hand. It crashes to the cement patio floor.

Mrs. Gallagher crouches forward. Her neck is red and swollen between her fingers.

"Mom!" I scream.

My mom reaches Mrs. Gallagher just in time for her to fall face first into my mom's feet.

"Mrs. Gallagher!" I cry.

"Call 911!" my mom yells.

She turns her over. Mrs. Gallagher's face is now a red, blotchy stretch of skin, her eyes bulging wide and her mouth pushed open by her tongue, which looks to be enormous. I stare mesmerized, and believe I will have this image burned in my memory for the rest of my life.

"Do it now!"

I break my gaze and run into the house. Grabbing the phone off the back counter, I dial 911.

"Dispatch. Is this an emergency?"

Yes. Yes, it is.

CHAPTER TWENTY

The End of the Yellow Brick Road

As soon as the paramedics arrive, I run out the front door, jump on my mom's bike and ride the Yellow Brick Road for all it's worth. No one needs to tell me Mrs. Gallagher has died. I know it. I saw her face before the ambulance showed up. She was dead when I got off the phone.

It was that fast.

My legs cramp, but I don't care. I continue to pedal as fast as I can. My vision is blurry but I don't dare take my hands off the handlebars to wipe away the tears. All I can think of is to go far, far away. As far as the path will take me.

It's HOT. Man, why didn't I throw a water bottle in the basket?

Mrs. Gallagher is dead.

I ride past the park and I hear somebody calling my name. Don't know, don't care. I cross a street and ride some more. I almost run into a car pulling out of the church parking lot.

I ride past the church, the cemetery, and Starbucks.

I ride and I ride and I ride until I am forced to stop at a light. Beyond it the road turns into a divided highway. The traffic is too heavy for me to continue. I am at the end of the Yellow Brick Road.

Why, God, why? Why did you have to kill her? I hate you! I'm never talking to you again!

My legs throb and my chest burns. I consider turning around and asking for water at Starbucks, but instead decide to turn back the way I came. I coast past Starbucks and ride into the cemetery where I don't stop until I find Mrs. Gallagher's blank stone. Once I find it, I let the bike fall over and I crawl off, sobbing. Between crying and being out of breath from the bike ride, my throat tightens up and I struggle to breathe. So this is what it feels like to have asthma, I think. Or how Mrs. Gallagher felt.

I try to get a handle on it by forcing myself to take deep breaths. As I sit hunched over the grave breathing like a yoga student, I look to my left and see the strangest thing: Beyond the back of the funeral building, past a nicely trimmed lawn, a man sits on a riding lawn mower, and he's waving at me.

It's the Caretaker from the other day. The one with the pearly whites.

It takes me a few seconds to realize he's not only waving at me, he's waving for me to come over. I wipe my eyes as I walk my mom's bike to the back of the funeral home and lean it against the building. He rides up alongside me and kills the motor.

"Why, greetings again!" he says, and he flashes me the warmest smile. For some reason his kindness makes me want to cry, and I go ahead and let it rip. I bury my head in my hands, and the next thing I know I have what feels like a large leather mitt on my shoulder. It's his hand. It feels strong and reassuring, not at all what I would imagine an old man's grip to be. I collapse into his arms and just cry and cry and cry. He smells like a campfire. That's the only way I can describe it. It smells good.

When I finally stop crying, he says, "There, now. What's the matter, sweetheart?"

"Mrs. Gallagher is dead."

"What?"

"It's true. And it was all my fault."

"Why don't you come inside and calm down. I'll get you a pop and we'll talk about it."

I nod and follow him inside. On my way to the back I notice the Harrison dude has left the building. The other rooms are still empty. Not for long.

I walk past his office and sit at one of the plastic tables in the alcove. Within a minute, the Caretaker returns with a Cream Soda and a paper towel.

"Sorry that took so long. I couldn't find any tissues, but this'll do." He hands me the soda and towel. He chuckles, "Of all the places to run outta Kleenex! I s'pose if it's good enough for those tough to clean spills, then . . . "

His voice trails off as he watches me drink the entire soda in practically one large swallow.

"You musta been thirsty. I'll get you another."

I smile politely. While he's gone, I look around. Wilted flowers are stuffed in vases on all the tables.

"What's your name, young lady?"

I'm startled to see the Caretaker directly in front of me with a second bottle of soda.

"Bitsy Johnson, thank you very much." I take the bottle from his hand, and a wave of gratitude washes over me.

"Bitsy. Is that a nickname?"

I nod. "For Elizabeth."

"Elizabeth. One of the classics. How did you go from Elizabeth to Bitsy?"

"My dad made it up when I was little. You know, after that song, 'The Itsy Bitsy Spider.'"

"Daddies love their little girls."

I hold the bottle against my forehead. The cold glass feels good on my skin. Some dads do.

"Now, do you want to tell me what happened?"

"Mrs. Gallagher was at our house this morning, walking our labyrinth."

"A labyrinth! You have a labyrinth?"

I nod.

"And Jean Gallagher was walking it?"

"It was her second time."

"Good for her."

The phone rings inside the back office.

"Bitsy, I'll be right back. You'll be okay, won't you?"

I smile and politely nod again.

"Wait right here. I want to hear what you have to say."

He walks inside the back office and as he takes the phone call, I hear the door open on the other side of the building.

"Bitsy?"

I peer around the corner of the alcove to see who's calling me, and I can't believe my eyes. It's Nick standing at the back door entrance.

"What are you doing?" I call out. When he sees me, he breaks into a run across the lobby.

"You were on a bike by the park. I yelled, but you just kept going."

Nick looks angry and relieved to see me at the same time.

"I couldn't find you!"

"I didn't know I was lost!"

"You weren't. I . . . It's just that . . . I don't know."

When he reaches me in the alcove, he does a slow wind-up and fake punches me in the arm. I smile at the clunky attempt at affection.

"So," he says, "Here you are." Nick eyes the bottle on the table and declares, "It is freakin' hot out there."

I smile, "You can have it."

He takes my soda and chugs it.

"Greetings, who do have we here?" The Caretaker says, locking the office door behind him.

"This is Nick."

Nick reaches out to shake the Caretaker's hand. "Nice to meet you, sir."

"The pleasure is mine."

The Caretaker heads to the back door so we follow him. "I just got a call from the hospital and I'm afraid you were right about Jean Gallagher. I need to go to the mortuary to prepare for her arrival."

For a few brief moments I forgot what had happened. I'm hit by a fresh batch of tears when I hear the news. "But I thought you cut lawns!" I cry, waving my two-ply paper towel.

He smiles, and I almost want to use my hand to shield me from the glare of those white teeth. "I'm a jack-of-all-trades, as they say."

I continue to silently cry when he puts a hand on my shoulder. "It's going to be okay, Bitsy. Trust me."

Nick and I follow the Caretaker out the door. Once outside, he says, "Kids, stay here as long as you have to. I'll be back in a little while." He pulls out a key ring from his pocket. "And remember what we talked about yesterday."

Was it just yesterday I wondered if his teeth were bought and paid for?

The man winks at me and jingles the keys. "Sometimes it takes time to comprehend God's purpose in things. Why, you may go your entire life and still not understand the meaning."

Nick and I listen intently.

"Th' point is, you should try to find peace within yourself. Not because of your circumstances, but despite them."

He disappears around the corner of the building and soon after backs out of the parking lot in a long, black Cadillac. It's the type that can easily double for a hearse, and I have no doubt that today it will be used for just this purpose.

"Son, can you make sure Bitsy makes it home safe and sound?" The Caretaker calls out.

"Yes, sir!"

The Caretaker waves at us one last time, and then he's gone.

Nick follows me as I grab my mom's bike, still leaning against the wall. I walk it toward the parking lot.

"Wait," he says, "Where are you going?"

"Time to pull the plug," I say, on a mission.

"Wha . . . can you at least tell me what happened?"

"Please leave me alone."

"But I told the guy I'd get you home." He tries to stop me by placing a hand over mine on the handlebar. I pull it back as if touching a flame.

"Don't touch me!" I cry, "I'm bad luck."

I keep moving. Nick skips to catch up again.

"Can I at least walk with you?"

"No. But I bet Josie's available. Her and her stupid glasses."

"Did you fall off your bike or something? You're not making any sense."

"I saw her splashing you at Gina's. She likes you."

"So?"

"See? You admit it!" I feel irrational but justified in saying this.

"Admit what? That Josie's a cling-on? So what?"

As I continue on, I begin to pick up speed. I throw a leg over the bike and hop on as it moves.

Nick calls out, "Wait! Tell me what happened!"

I call over my shoulder, "I have to do something first!"

I look back one last time and see Nick standing there, watching me ride away. The memory I want so desperately to forget rises to the surface. Again, I push it down. Hopefully for good this time. I will not let it be played. I repeat, I will *not* let it be played.

CHAPTER TWENTY ONE

Flames

I CLOSE THE side gate behind me and march to the tool shed. I step inside and look for the gasoline container. It's exactly where I left it last week when I moved it away from the lavender. I grab it and walk to the door before I can change my mind. The container feels heavier than the last time I held it. Its contents slosh from side to side as I stomp toward the labyrinth.

I stop short when I see someone sitting on the labyrinth. At first I think it's the ghost of Mrs. Gallagher, and I get spooked a little. But the more I look, the more I realize that not only is it *not* the ghost of Mrs. Gallagher, it's someone

I'd never in a million years expect to be anywhere *near* the labyrinth.

It's Ellen.

She sits in the center of the maze, holding a square glass bottle to her lips. She drinks until it's practically upside down, draining it. "Stop it!" I scream. I run toward her.

Ellen jumps and then stands. For a second it looks like she's going to fall back down, but then she just staggers a little and looks at me with these small slits for eyes. When she sees it's me, her eyes narrow even more.

"Don't look at me like that!" I shout. I drop the container and plow right into her. We fall together. Her bottle slides out of her hand and shatters on the ground.

"Get off of it!" I say, rolling off of her.

"Ow! You're crazy." Ellen checks her arm. It's cut in several places. Blood oozes from the largest gash.

Out of breath, I stand and wipe myself off. Then I go back for the container. Once I have it, I uncap the lid. Sweat drips off my nose as I shake the smelly liquid onto the labyrinth.

"What are you doing? Hey!" Ellen jumps off the labyrinth just as gasoline splashes nearby. She doesn't dare go near me as I empty the container in the middle.

I feel completely crazy and uncontrollable, like I'm having an out of body experience. It feels magnificent. I smile at Ellen and stumble backward, feeling around for something in my pocket.

When I reach the edge, I jump off and show Ellen my pocket's contents: a book of matches.

"No!" she shouts.

Too late. I strike a match and throw it on the labyrinth. The gasoline bursts into flames. We're on opposite sides of the labyrinth, Ellen and me, separated by fire.

"Bitsy!" she shrieks.

I come to my senses when I see the blaze, and start to panic when the fire laps at the surrounding plants. It quickly takes the neighboring bushes. Then the wooden flower containers. They crackle and burn.

I look beyond the labyrinth at the patio. The patio that's attached to our house. They seem awfully close to the fire. I look back at the blaze and see the fire moving from shrub to shrub. Even the grass ignites, and I have the random thought that it's because of the dry, hot weather.

I run toward the house and turn the spigot knob at the wall. I follow the uncoiled garden hose to Ellen, who's dragging it behind her. When she nears the flames, she plants herself and turns on the hose. A small stream of water gushes out before going dry.

"Bitsy!" she yells at me, "turn back on the water!"

In my confusion, I must've turned the spigot off after Ellen had already turned it on!

Ellen takes a step backward as the fire moves out in every direction. "Bitsy!" she shrieks, "Hurry!"

I quickly crank the handle, and within seconds a stream of water sprays out of the hose that Ellen has positioned in front of the fire.

I linger at the house and watch the action. It feels like forever but within minutes she has it contained. When Ellen douses the last of the flames, I slowly walk back to the labyrinth.

As I reach her, Ellen lets the hose hang, then

fall off her limp hand. Coughing, she says, "And you thought smoking was bad?"

She leans over and holds her knees as she tries to recover. I survey the damage: Everything surrounding the labyrinth is blackened and burned. And yet—

The labyrinth remains unscathed.

☙

LATER, AFTER COUNTLESS threats and many insults thrown at me by my sister, I stand on the labyrinth with a broom and trash bin. The same bin I tried to hide the rank evidence in last weekend. I sweep glass into a heavy duty dustpan and drop the shards in the container. Smoke hangs in the air as I wipe sweat off my neck.

God, I'm so tired. My life's a mess.

I squeeze my eyes shut. I didn't mean to pray like that! I'm still not speaking to God. It's like when you're mad at someone and you forget you're mad and you go to call them on the phone, and then you remember: Hey! I'm mad at her! Only it's much harder with God, because all you have to do is think of Him and you're kinda praying. And He reads minds. This is really tricky.

I put my hands up to my ears and say, "LA LA LA LA LA LA LA" to try to block out any communication. I don't want to talk to God and I certainly don't want Him talking to me.

"LA LA LA LA LA LA." It's official: I'm a *bona fide* crazy person.

CHAPTER TWENTY TWO

Making Amends

I SIT AT the mouth of the labyrinth with my knees tucked into my chest and my arms wrapped around my knees. My stomach growls because I never had breakfast or lunch and now it's almost dinnertime.

"Bitsy."

My mom's walking toward me from the patio. When she spots the damage, she hesitates. Seeing her look so sad and disappointed makes me choke up. I caused this. All of it.

"Sweetie, you okay?" she asks. She reaches me and crouches down to my eye level.

I nod my head because I'm afraid my voice will crack if I try to speak.

"Ellen told me what happened."

"I'm really sorry."

"She cut her arm pretty bad," my mom says, brushing a piece of hair away from my face. "Fortunately they're just surface cuts, nothing that will require stitches."

"Did she say how she cut it?" I ask.

"She was rather vague, but I know it had something to do with a bottle of Schnapps. I thought you'd fill in the blanks for me."

I shrug. The last thing I'm going to do is rat out my sister.

"I see," she says, taking a seat next to me. "Well, now it's her turn to be grounded. I really hope you two got this drinking business out of your systems."

We sit in silence for a minute, looking at the labyrinth. Finally she asks, "Why'd you do it?"

I shrug again.

"Are you that unhappy? I thought we built a pretty good life here."

"She died because of me. I tried to stop it before it happened again." I brush away a tear.

"Honey, you don't have that kind of power. None of us do. Please don't feel responsible for something that wasn't your fault."

"Are you mad at me?"

"Am I mad at you," she repeats, as if turning over the question in her mind. "Yeah, I'm mad at you. You lied to me about your father for reasons I have yet to understand, you ran off without telling me where you were going and for how long you'd be gone, and then you set fire to our property. So, yes, I'm angry about those things."

I hug my knees to my chest even tighter.

"But I'm also mad at myself."

I raise an eye to meet hers. She continues, "It's obvious you don't feel comfortable sharing things with me, and I'm sad I allowed that to happen. Ellen told me you complained I've been gone so much."

"I swear she is such . . . "

My mom holds up a hand to stop me. "She is *concerned*, is what she is. You've been trying to tell me, too, but I was too busy to listen."

I shrug again. "I guess so."

"What I'm trying to say is that I'm sorry. I'm going to do better. I promise."

I smile weakly at my mom. I want to believe her, really I do.

"Bitsy, you back here?"

It's Gina calling me from the side of our garage. My mom slowly rises to her feet and waves for Gina to join us. She says to me, "I came out to tell you Gina called. She's coming by for a quick visit. Guess I got a little side tracked."

I chuckle. She adds before Gina gets to us, "I'll be in the house making dinner if you need anything."

"I thought you were going out."

"Not anymore."

When Gina approaches, my mom hugs her tightly. "I'm so sorry," she says to Gina, and Gina nods in gratitude.

I jump to my feet, and when it's my turn to hug Gina I give her a big squeeze and she breaks down. "She's gone, I can't believe she's gone," she sobs. "I knew she was going to die, but like this?!"

My mom brushes away a tear as she makes her way back to the patio.

We break from our hug. "It happened so fast, I couldn't stop it," I say. "I'm so sorry."

Gina wipes away tears, and then pulls out a packet of tissues from her pocket. "I didn't know what else to do, so I thought I'd walk your laby-rinth. Maybe I'll feel my mom here," she eyes me for approval. "I asked on the phone and she said it'd be okay."

"Yeah. Sure. Of course it's okay."

I start to say more when I see her look beyond me, at the labyrinth and the charred remains.

"What happened?" she asks.

"It's a super long story."

CHAPTER TWENTY THREE

Pray to Change Me

MY MOM MAKES our favorite meal: steak, baked potatoes, salad, and cinnamon apples. She brings a large bread basket to the kitchen table and sits to eat with us. I surprise myself and wolf down the food like a refugee. Even Ellen notices.

"Slow down, stupid! You'll choke," she says, holding her head in one hand and picking a tomato off her salad with the other.

"What do you care? You want me dead anyway."

"If I wanted you dead, I'd've let you burn to death." Ellen stabs some romaine and eats it.

"That's enough," my mom says. "I don't want to hear any more fighting."

We eat in silence, no doubt thinking about the events of the day. I creep a small smile, and say, "I'm sorry I set the backyard on fire."

Ellen grins. "And I'm sorry you're my sister, but what are we going to do?"

The phone rings.

"I'll get it!" I say, jumping up.

My mom says, "If it's for me, tell them I'll call them back later."

That's different, I think. I pick up the phone on the third ring. "Hello?"

"Bitsy?"

"Daddy!"

I grin at Ellen and turn my back to them so I can speak privately.

"You sound so good," my dad says. "I miss you, Honey."

"I miss you too!"

"I got the picture you e-mailed me. You're all grown up!"

"That's what kids do, Dad. We grow."

"Best to send those to my work address." He laughs sheepishly. "Our internet is so messed up here."

I'm quiet for a minute as I see the situation for

what it is: I'm part of his old life. It's that simple. I'm being phased out. "Sure. No problem-o," I say.

"I don't have much time to talk, but I need to tell you . . . "

"Lemme guess. You have to cancel again."

"Here's the thing."

"Don't worry about it. We're busy anyway with Mom's lavender festival."

"A festival? Sounds like fun."

A dull throb forms in the back of my head. The memory. Here it comes.

"Look, I gotta go," I stammer. "Mom made a nice meal and dinner's getting cold."

"Well, let's reschedule."

I look over at my mom, at Ellen. They're watching me, hearing my side of the conversation. The memory comes back in Technicolor. I talk into the phone while keeping eye contact with Ellen. "Why don't you send me an e-mail and I'll look at my calendar."

Ellen grins.

My dad laughs but there's a crack in his voice. "You are definitely becoming the teenager everybody warned me about."

"How would you know?"

"My itsy spider wouldn't . . . "

I interrupt him. "Look, Dad. I love you, but I gotta run."

Before he can respond, I hang up and drop the phone into its cradle.

The memory comes back with force and this time I don't stop it. I hear it, see it, and smell it as if it's happening at this very minute. My memory is this: I'm nine years old and sitting at our old kitchen table back in California. My mom's making dinner and my sister's in the other room, watching T.V. My dad's home early from work for reasons I can't remember. He's sitting at the table with me and we're playing UNO, waiting for dinner to be ready. My mom's breaking salad into bits and placing them in four bowls, and we're laughing because my dog, Chip, is playing fetch with an old knotted towel, and no matter how many times my dad interrupts the game to throw the towel, Chip is there within seconds to drop the slobbery mess at my feet. I'm perfectly content. I don't want anything. It's just a normal day, and we love each other.

I let the feelings wash over me. It was the last day I remember our family being happy together.

"You're awfully quiet," my mom says, putting a hand on my shoulder.

"It's been a long day."

She steals a look at me, and says, "I love you, Sweetie Pie."

I bury my head in her arms and cry.

CR

LATER, AFTER WE'VE finished dinner and I've cleared away all the dishes, I walk outside to find Ellen. My mom's getting ready to go see that lady in the next town. She's going to tell her tonight that she needs to spend more time with us. I really do want to believe her. After all, she did make dinner.

I find Ellen near the apiary. She leans against the shed, listening to the bees buzzing in the bee boxes nearby.

"Are you looking for the one that killed Mrs. Gallagher?" I say.

"It's dead already. They die after they sting."

"I knew that. I was just seeing if you knew that."

"Right."

It's almost eight o' clock at night, and it's still pushing ninety degrees. The only noise around us is the low hum of the bees working in their hives.

"I'm sorry I pushed you. I didn't mean it."

Ellen doesn't say anything, but instead stares at the bee boxes.

"I heard Gina came over tonight."

"Yeah."

"I'm surprised, considering her mom was just there this morning."

"You were sitting in the middle of it this afternoon and it didn't seem to bother you."

"I was seeing if God had anything to say."

"And?"

Ellen shakes her head and watches the bees. "I've never been stung. I don't know why. I know you have."

"Mom's been stung a gazillion times."

"Right. I wonder what's in me that makes 'em want to stay away."

"I bet if you put your hand in there they would."

She continues, "It's kinda like the deal I've got going with God. The whole 'not praying,' it's kinda like, I don't bother Him, and He won't bother me.

Don't get me wrong, I've gotta healthy respect that He's there and all. But I just figure, people pray for stuff all the time and it doesn't happen."

She pauses, and then says, "So if He doesn't get involved . . . why should I?"

"Are you kidding me?" I exclaim, "He's a big, fat busy body if you ask me."

Ellen grins, still looking at the bee boxes. "I'm thinking now that maybe I was wrong not to pray because I couldn't change things. I think I was supposed to pray to change *me*."

"Even though you might get stung?"

She shrugs and we chuckle. "I made some Break n Bakes. Want one?" I add, enticingly, "Chocolate chip."

She smiles and nods and we walk into the house together.

CHAPTER TWENTY FOUR

The Trouble with Nick

Mrs. Gallagher's funeral is a circus. Being a Realtor, she must've known half the town. Gina and I hang out and text people while we wait. My mom and Ellen arrive together, and I'm touched that Ellen showed. Then again, after last Tuesday's escapade, my mom hasn't let Ellen out of her sight. I spot Josie with her mom by the ashtray cans at the back of the funeral home. Josie looks miserable as her mom chain smokes and talks to one of Josie's former teachers. Dylan and Nick help arrange the plastic folding chairs on the cemetery lawn. Today is supposed to be the beginning of our weekend Lavender Festival, but my mom canceled today out of respect for

Mrs. Gallagher. It's too bad. The heat wave has finally broken, and it's a perfect Oregon summer day: low-eighties and partly cloudy.

I watch my mom and Ellen greet Mr. Gallagher near the funeral home. After he moves on to shake hands with other people, I notice my mom looking down her nose at Josie. I cringe and go back to my texting.

The Gallagher family had a viewing in the funeral parlor for one day only, yesterday, and even then it wasn't really a viewing because it was a closed casket. That was on account of the fact that Mrs. Gallagher's face got so swollen when she died that they thought it would freak everybody out to see her like that. Instead, they had a framed poster-sized picture of her propped up on an easel next to the casket. It must've been her Realtor photo from the glossy magazines because it was professionally done and she was all "BLINGed" out. The weirdest thing about yesterday was seeing the name GALLAGHER on the front of the funeral room door. It was a different room from the Harrison person. I was glad about that. Otherwise, it would've felt like a revolving door.

Nick sidles up to me. I drop my phone in the grass. As I go to pick it up, he says, "Hey."

I offer a witty reply: "Hey."

"Can you help me get a couple more chairs?" he asks.

"Okaayy."

I follow Nick into the funeral home. Gina giggles as we leave together.

As I make my way out of the supply room with two chairs under my arms, I peek in on the chapel room. Inside, alone at the front pew, kneels the Caretaker. He slowly gets up, hat in hand, and walks to the candles. Bowing his head, he lights one.

I turn to head outside when I run directly into Nick.

"Oh!"

"Here," he says, "Let me get those."

He takes the chairs from me and I shyly head for the door.

"Wait."

I hesitate. Nick awkwardly holds the chairs as he steps closer to block me from leaving. I look into his eyes. We're body to body, but the chairs prevent us from getting too close. A surge of electricity runs through me and I am frozen in the moment.

"Why haven't you called me back?" he asks.

"We're working overtime for the festival."

"Josie said you canceled."

My guard instantly goes up when I hear her name.

"Only for today. We're back on tomorrow and Sunday."

"Oh."

"Look," I say, "I gotta go." I shoot past him and almost make it to the doors, when—

"Wait."

I stop again, but now I'm irritated.

He begins, "I tried to tell you the other day . . . "

"I know, Josie's a cling-on. Fine."

"I don't like Josie!"

"You don't?"

"What I was trying to say is I like somebody else!"

"You do?"

"Yeah, and she's a real pain in the ass, too. Did you know that?"

My legs feel like water as he leans into me to say the last part. I bite my lip and try to hide the smile that's beginning to form on my face. With my back, I push open the double doors to go outside. Nick stumbles but recovers.

"Hey!" he calls, "I just told you I liked someone else!"

I smile and look back one last time. "She likes you too!"

I can't believe I just said that! I continue on, reliving my words in my mind, and thinking about Nick, standing in the doorway with chairs in his hands, looking like he just hit Teen Lotto.

CHAPTER TWENTY FIVE

A Revelation

Soft music begins to play, and all the people who'd been milling around take seats. Everyone speaks in hushed tones. A few of Mrs. Gallagher's relatives look around disapprovingly. Gina said that the last-minute decision to have the funeral outdoors was not popular with some of the old people.

Nick sits down next to me and my family, and I think I am going to officially die when he takes my hand in his. Instead of pulling away like before, this time I let him hold it. He squeezes my hand and even though I feel lousy about Mrs. Gallagher, I am positively melting into my plastic fold up chair. He smiles at me. "How about after the funeral I come over and help you set up for the festival? I can move tables, sweep floors, massage shoulders."

"Thanks, I'm sure my mom would love that. The helping part! Not the shoulders." I take a breath. "Okay, let's say that again."

Nick laughs. "I got it."

I am about to make yet another witty comment, like "Yeah," or "Okay," when we hear a loud commotion at the entrance of the cemetery. Everyone stands and my mom does a double take. A woman leans against the open gate. Ellen and I exchange looks.

"Oh, no," my mom says, "It's Susan."

I whisper to her, "I thought you said she had sixty days?"

Susan staggers forward, cups her eyes to ward off the glare, and looks into the crowd.

She calls out, "Amy? You here?" She walks mostly on the sides of her high heels. Her makeup is smeared under her eyes and her buttons aren't lined up on her blouse. I can only imagine how much she had to drink to look this way.

My mom looks mortified. "I tell her to start

looking for a new sponsor and she pulls this. I'm sorry, Honey. I have to go help her."

Here we go again, I think. I try to hide my disappointment but all I can do is nod. My mom gets up and moves toward the woman. Ellen follows closely behind.

I watch my mom try to put a hand on Susan's shoulder. She pulls away, stumbles slightly backwards, but recovers.

"Don't you touch me!" she slurs.

My mom says something quietly to her, to which she responds loudly, "Whadda you care? They're with their father, the Disney Dad. He, who can do no wrong!"

My mom tries again and this time successfully leads Susan out of the gate. Ellen has her arm on the other side. When they're out of sight, I fixate my eyes on the casket and try not to feel hurt that my mom has to leave yet again during an event that's so important to me.

The Pastor begins the service by walking to the front of the crowd, next to the casket. "Thank you for joining us as we celebrate the life of Mary Jean Gallagher. Let us pray to the Lord."

While the pastor says his "Our Father" prayer, I say my own version: *God, I do need you. I act like I don't, but I do.* I steal a look at Nick and his head is bowed in prayer.

I pause, and study the back of the chair in front of me. The black plastic is scuffed in spots, and on the bottom, someone has spray-stenciled the words PROPERTY OF HOPE COMMUNITY CHURCH. I close my eyes and try to focus on the Pastor's words.

Someone brushes past me and I when I look up, I'm astonished to see my mom retaking her seat. She squeezes my leg before locking her own hands in prayer. As I hear my mom recite the prayer, I squeeze my eyes shut and practically giggle out my words. Afterward, my mom leans to me and whispers, "The nice man who works here is going to wait until the cab arrives. I asked Ellen to stay in case he needed help. It's a good service opportunity."

I can feel myself grinning from cheek to cheek.

At the urging of the Pastor, the crowd stands. My mom puts an arm around me. I finish my prayer:

Thank you for my mom. I know she tries to help You and she's doing the best job she can. I know she does it gladly because when You're happy, she's happy. I think I'm beginning to figure this out. Please look after my dad and Coco, I mean, Charlene. I hope she loves him as much as I do. Thank you also for Nick. He's such a great guy. Thank you for reaching Ellen. Finally, please, please, please help Gina and her family cope with losing her mom. I know she's with You now, and I just ask that Mrs. Gallagher be a kind of Guardian Angel now to all of us.

I glance over at Nick. He must sense it because he winks at me. I quickly go back to my prayer: *Let me restate that. I don't want Mrs. Gallagher watching over me all of the time. Especially when I am with Nick. Thank you, Amen.*

The rest of the service seems like a dream to me. Mrs. Gallagher has a gazillion friends who have nice things to say about her. Mr. Gallagher doesn't speak, but judging by the look on his face, I can tell he appreciates what's being said. I look around and notice the Caretaker now stands at the back of the crowd. Our eyes meet and he tips his cap to me. I turn back and smile.

Afterward, Dylan, Nick, Josie and I help fold chairs and carry them across the lawn and into the storage room behind the funeral parlor. By the time we get to the last of the chairs, the cemetery is empty again. I decide to run back to the gravesite one more time before I catch up with the others. When I get there, the Caretaker is removing flowers from the top of Mrs. Gallagher's casket.

"Greetings, again, Bitsy. It was a nice service, don't you think?"

"Yes, very nice." I check out the flowers. "Those are beautiful."

"Why, thank you. I arranged 'em m'self."

I laugh, "You really are a jack-of-all-trades!"

The Caretaker grins and his teeth practically radiate. "Strange, isn't it? How she died, that is."

"Who would have guessed?"

"Maybe she did. After all, her sister died the same way."

I am stunned. "What do you mean?" I ask.

"She was in here the other day, talking 'bout her arrangements, I asked her how her sister had come to pass, and she told me she'd been stung by a bee."

"Mrs. Gallagher knew she was allergic?"

The Caretaker shakes his head. "She never knew for sure. Said she didn't want to find out the hard way."

"That's amazing," I say, almost to myself. I study Rita Brown's headstone, Resident Dead Person and Bee Sting Recipient Number One. I look up to ask the Caretaker another question, but he's gone.

Nick approaches with Josie in tow. Great.

"Ready to go?" Nick asks me.

I shake my head. "I'll catch up with you guys later. My mom and I need to get back."

Josie smiles smugly at me. "Fine by us. C'mon, Nick."

"Uh, that's okay," Nick says. "I'm going to do my own thing."

Josie clenches her fist a little. She offers up a fake smile, and says, "What was I thinking? I can't hang with you. I have my mom here."

Nick smiles and raises one of his trademark guppy eyebrows at me.

CHAPTER TWENTY SIX

Community

A N HOUR AFTER THE funeral, I'm standing alone with my mom at the base of the
labyrinth. Together, we look at the burnt sur-
roundings.

She says, "I have absolutely no idea how we can
fix this by tomorrow."

"Doesn't look very festive, does it."

"For Halloween, maybe."

"We can string some twinkle lights on the dead
branches."

"Guess we'll just have to tell everyone the
truth."

I grimace. "Great. I'm going to forever be
labeled the pyro-freak."

My mom gives me a squeeze. I look back at the back gate and see Nick and Dylan letting themselves in. I wave to them.

"Might as well get started," my mom says, "I'll get my work clothes . . . "

My mom hesitates when she sees what I see: More people are walking in behind Nick and Dylan.

She states, "They must think we're having the festival today."

I sincerely freak since we are completely unprepared. "What are we going to do?" I ask.

As the crowd moves closer, I notice the women are carrying casseroles and other food dishes. The men are hauling plant containers, buckets, rakes and brooms. At the front of the crowd is the Caretaker. He reaches my mom first.

"Heard you could use a hand," he says to her jovially.

He motions for the men to join him near the labyrinth. The men move past him, drop off their work items, and circle the labyrinth admiringly. The Caretaker winks at me and moves on.

Women come forward with their dishes. Gina is there and she's holding flowers.

"Everyone wanted to see it," says Gina.

Her dad steps forward and nods to the women with food. "Jean must've talked this place up because her church group has just brought lunch."

The place is beginning to look like a cross between a wake and a Habitat for Humanity event. My mom and I look around in amazement at the spontaneous gathering. The men take great care to stay off the labyrinth as they remove dead bushes and position new plants.

A few of the women move to the opening of the labyrinth and step forward on its path.

Dylan stares at the labyrinth as if it's from outer space. "Dude!" he says, "This thing is so Monster House!"

Nick smiles and says to me, "Whatever *that* means."

My mom nods toward Josie and her mom walking through the gate, and says to me, "I'm going to have a word with Josie's mom later to let her know I do *not* approve."

OMG!

My mom tugs on my hand. "Walk with me, Sweetie Pie?"

I relax and squeeze her hand. Together, we step on the labyrinth.

My mom gently guides me onto the narrow path before us.

Just a quickie to say, thanks, God, and if you need anything, just let me know. I'm happy to help out in any way I can. I watch the crowds, moving off the labyrinth and toward the patio, where the conversation is becoming louder and livelier. *I suppose this beats a swimming pool, hands down, but it would've been nice. Especially with that heat wave. Just kidding. This'll do just fine.*

I look up at the sky and wonder if Mrs. Gallagher is watching us. Probably not. She's probably already checking out the real estate, looking for the perfect view. After all, she is the Perfect Realtor, you know.

THE END

Book Group
Discussion Questions

1. Which character in *Bitsy's Labyrinth* did you identify with the most, and why?

2. As a sibling, are you more like Bitsy or more like Ellen?

3. What are some of the problems that Bitsy faces at the beginning of the book? Are these problems resolved at the end of the story?

4. How would you have approached Bitsy's problems? What would you have done differently?

5. What was the role of the Caretaker?

6. Why do you think Bitsy's mom spent time helping other alcoholics?

7. What role did the labyrinth play in the story?

8. How did the labyrinth affect: Bitsy? Gina? Mrs. Gallagher? Ellen?

9. How does Bitsy's father change throughout the book, if at all?

10. How did you react when you found out Mrs. Gallagher's sister Rita also died from a bee sting?

11. How, if at all, does God respond to Bitsy's prayers?

Finger Labyrinth

A FINGER LABYRINTH IS a labyrinth that you trace with your finger. It works the same way as a walking labyrinth except you trace the path to the center using your finger instead of your feet.

Start at the opening and slowly move through the labyrinth as you pray or meditate. Notice your breathing as you "walk" the path. See if you can stretch the time it takes to reach the end. Peace be with you!

Acknowledgments

Thank you, Craig, for always being my first reader. I love you.

Thanks to early readers and supporters Anne Zoormajian, Colette Chatterton, Piper Olmsted, Bonnie Talbot, Kathy Young, Debbie Adams, Cameron Adams, Jill Ivie, Norene Quam, Paul McGee, Bill Johnson, Christina Katz, Nancy Froeschle, James Loos, Gibran Peron, Julie Fast, Claire Toland, and Emily Bostrom.

Much gratitude goes to Sarah Bader, owner of Lavender at Stonegate in West Linn, Oregon. You can find all things lavender at www.lavenderatstonegate.com

I am deeply indebted to Jennifer Omner at www.ALLPublications.com and Clark Kohanek at www.ClarkKohanek.com for creating the book's interior layout and exterior design. Your expertise gave my words beauty and meaning.

Thanks to Andrea Brown and Laura Rennert at the Andrea Brown Literary Agency for supporting the early manuscript. Thank you Jesse Lawler for believing that *Bitsy's Labyrinth* should be made into a movie.

A heaping thanks to publisher, agent and friend, April Eberhardt. Without you Bitsy would've lived out her days in a drawer.

I'm forever grateful to Pastor Kip Jacob at Southlake Church for blessing *Bitsy's Labyrinth,* and inspiring me and countless others with messages of faith and service.

And to my daughters Andi and Julia, I love you both very much.

MARY ANDONIAN WAS born and raised in Southgate, Michigan. She graduated from Eastern Michigan University and earned an MBA from the University of Toledo. She enjoys playing Scrabble, reading and writing screenplays, and serving on the Board of Willamette Writers, one of the largest writers' associations in the United States. She lives in the Pacific Northwest with her husband, two daughters, and two cats. Visit Mary at www.maryandonian.com

Breinigsville, PA USA
04 January 2011
252587BV00005B/1/P